The Long Journey of Joslin de Lay

Book 6

THE FALSE FATHER

Dennis Hamley

JOSLIN BOOKS

The six books which comprise *The Long Journey of Joslin de Lay s* were first published in the UK by Scholastic Ltd between 1998 and 2001.

The False Father was first published in.2001 This new paperback edition was published in 2018 by **JOSLIN BOOKS (Oxford, UK).**

ISBN 978-1-9998151-8-9

Cover image and design by Anastasia Sichkarenko

JOSLIN BOOKS is the imprint under which Dennis Hamley's new compilations of stories, reissues of previously published books and books not intended for other publishers will appear.

The Long Journey of Joslin de Lay was written in memory of Tony Gibbs (1938 – 1966) of Falmouth, Jesus College, Cambridge and Langwith College, York, who loved the Middle Ages, would have been one of the greatest of scholars and writers about the medieval world and who wrote a wonderful book about the ballads Joslin sings.

CONTENTS

PART ONE

1351

A Father's Tale

1

The year was 1351, four years before the great Battle of Poitiers, where the English army would rout the flower of French knighthood. The place was a small town in Normandy, in the north of France. A young travelling minstrel was playing his songs in the market-place and scores of townsfolk had gathered to listen.

Suddenly, from a watchtower in the walls, a shrill, cracked bell tolled, strident and urgent. Now, no one was listening to the minstrel. This was the alarm bell. A fearful cry went up from the crowd. "The English. The English are coming."

A watchman on the tower shouted. "Be calm. It's not the English. Those are not English banners."

The minstrel felt relief wrap him round like a warm blanket. How terrible, to be set on by English hordes in his own country.

Another shout came from the tower. But this one ended in a scream of panic. "It's not the English. *It's Yvain de Galles.*"

The minstrel knew who the watchman meant. Yvain de Galles as the French called him – Owain of Wales, Owain of the Red Hand or Owain Lawgoch as he was known in his own country. He was far worse than any Englishman, because he was a favourite of King Philip of France and King James after him, and they let him do what he liked. If that meant roaming the land with his band of renegade Welshmen, looting and pillaging towns and villages, well, why should kings and nobles care? People living there were only peasants. As if being half wiped out by the Black Death hadn't been enough. It mattered nothing as long as Owain Lawgoch would help the king of France against the hated English.

Outside was a loud galloping of hooves and yelling of men. Through the town gates the invaders poured. The fight was short. Even as the minstrel watched, the burning and killing started. The townsfolk tried to flee and hide. Some succeeded. Those who failed lay dead and wounded: the minstrel heard dying cries as he stood powerless, waiting his turn. Women were dragged away. Their screams mingled with terrified squeals of pigs, and roars of cattle being killed.

But the minstrel's turn never came. A small, dark, wiry man seized him with sword upraised. Then he saw the tunic and the harp. He lowered his sword, smiled and said in French with a strange accent, "A minstrel, eh? Then you'll come back with us. Owain will be pleased. You'll remind him of his days in the court of King Philip."

Though small, he man was immensely strong. The minstrel had no chance has he was bundled was bundled away to a place well hidden by trees away where even now a great tent was being erected and dark wiry men stood waiting, all armed and many bloodstained and still panting with the effort of killing.

The tent was finished and full of warlike men. The young minstrel began to play his harp with trembling fingers. He drew breath, nearly retched again with the horror of what he had seen, then sang. His voice shook.

"Louder," cried the soldier sitting at the head of the tent. "I want a song of triumph to tell all France that Owain Lawgoch, Owain of the Red Hand, does what he likes and the king of France is pleased to let him."

That was the pity of it, thought the minstrel. This man had done great things already for the king of France. He and his little band far from home fought the English like tigers. Who could blame them? They hated the English as much as any Frenchman did. The English had conquered Wales and King Edward's castles blotted their fair land. If Edward had his way, soon France would be under his heel as well. So these men had left Wales and joined King Edward's sworn enemies.

There was no point now in Welshmen trying to fight the English in Wales. One day perhaps. Not yet. Things were different in France, though, where English armies devastated towns and villages and where a new French king sat in Paris wondering what to do about it. Meanwhile, Owain and his Welshmen could roam the countryside looking for plunder and pick off a few English here and there as well.

What did the young French minstrel know about Owain's history? That he was descended from Owain, Prince of Gwynedd two hundred years before, that he possessed lands in England and Wales but had been brought up in the court of the French King Philip, that when Philip died a few months before he had quietly left and taken to being – what? Soldier? Robber? Brigand? Whichever was most convenient at the time. All this the minstrel had picked up on his travels across France, from whispers in corners from fearful people: "*Beware Yvain de Galles.*"

Now he was meeting him in his tent, at the head of a long table, with his men on each side. The great leader sat on a chair covered in furs, with crossed banners behind it, one of France, the other bearing a red dragon. At his shoulder stood another man, with a sallow face and dark hair, smiling as if at some private joke but seeming ready to pour thoughts and advice into the leader's ear. The minstrel had a sudden intuition that in this gathering this man was perhaps the most important.

The minstrel looked again at the leader and was surprised. Owain Lawgoch was such a young man – perhaps not twenty, hardly more than a boy – with a freckled face and freckles on the backs of his hands. Was that why he was called Owain of the Red Hand – a few freckles?

"Sing for us, minstrel," said Owain. His voice was high, almost like a boy's. His French was perfect, like a native.

The minstrel started a song of Roland, thinking that Owain might like being compared with such a great warrior. As he sang, Owain and his men ate vast mounds of looted beef, mutton and poultry and drank huge quantities of wine. The minstrel watched and thought on what often puzzled him. What he had seen in the town was terrible, but not surprising. This was how armies lived. Fighting *for* the king seemed to mean fighting *against* the people. He knew the English would loot the countryside. But these men were on France's side yet they were allowed to loot as well. There must be a better way than this.

The song ended. The Welshmen cheered and slapped him on the back. "Well sung," said Owain. "You've deserved your supper."

The minstrel was hungry. Plundered food was as wholesome as any other. As he ate, he had a strange thought. Owain might be Welsh. But he didn't speak Welsh and his French sounded like a Frenchman's. Yet these tough, rough Welshmen obeyed him unquestioningly and seemed to adore him.

As the minstrel ate, Owain watched him approvingly. The sallow-faced man at Owain's shoulder also watched him. But he looked at him differently, as if summing him up.

"My lord," he said at last, "minstrels are at home wherever they go. They are welcomed by both the highest and the lowest in any land."

"That's true, James," said Owain.

"They can speak to anybody and they'll always get an answer."

"I know."

"Even a Frenchman with songs to sing would be welcome in England, and even more so in Wales."

7

"What are you saying, James?"

"Here is your messenger – the one to take your question to the Welsh people and bring back their answer," the man replied.

"By God, you're right," Owain shouted.

"But if he's going to take a question, it's only fair that he knows for himself what that question is," said the man.

"We'll see." Owain clapped the minstrel on the shoulder. "Let me ask you something minstrel. Who is the Prince of Wales?"

"Why, the Black Prince, of course," the minstrel answered. "King Edward's son, and the scourge of all France, who's made many Frenchwomen widows before their time."

"I knew you'd say that," roared Owain delightedly. "Well, let me tell you this. The Black Prince is Prince of Wales through treacherous conquest. He's not Welsh. He hates Wales. He's never been there and he never will. There's only one man on God's earth who is Prince of Wales by right, whose claim no one can deny. Do you know who the true Prince of Wales is?"

The minstrel thought the best answer was a silent, intense interested look. *I'll wager you've not been to Wales either,* he thought.

"*I am,*" Owain thundered. "I'm directly descended from the true Welsh princes. One day I'll clear Wales of the English and I'll take my rightful place, so that no English king will dare take arms against me. They don't call me Owain of the Red Hand for nothing."

The minstrel thought that silence was still the best reply.

"The poets all say so," Owain continued. "For years, the bards have sung of a leader who will rise to take Wales back and return it to the Welsh. He will come from far away, yet everybody will know he's one of the princes of old. All true Welshmen will follow him."

There was complete silence in the tent.

"And the bards say his name will be Owain. Yvain in French, Owain in Welsh. I am the last of the Princes of Gwynedd, and I am that Owain which the bards prophesy. My father is dead, our lands have been taken unlawfully away and King Edward knows me as his sworn enemy. He is sure I will return one day, and the thought frightens him."

The minstrel found it hard to believe King Edward of England could fear this youth and his Welsh followers. But anything Owain said was believed in this tent. The men cheered, loud and ear-splitting: then voices were raised in a melody which seemed to start in pitch and time as if from one many-throated singer. The tune was free and wandering. The minstrel had never heard its like before and it made his ears tingle with its beauty. For a moment this crew, stained with blood and sweat, had become angels singing anthems.

Owain listened but did not join in. When he raised a hand, the singing died at once. He spoke again.

"Just one thing makes me pause. After years of English rule, perhaps my people have gone soft. Some are rich with English money. Some have taken high rank in England. Some are happy with the way things are. Why, many brave but deluded Welshmen are fighting for Edward now. It wasn't the English who beat the French at Crécy, it was the Welsh with their wicked bows and arrows." He laughed. "Strange. I hate what they did and who they did it for with my whole being, but I'm proud of how they did it. The Welsh had to teach the English how to fight. And now they're teaching the French."

There was an ironic cheer from the men. Owain raised his hand for silence. "I've seen what happens when a man rules a land which doesn't want him. Cruelty and murder, that's what. I love my people too much for that to happen to them. So do my countrymen want me? Are they content with their new lot? Do they want a Prince of Wales who's truly Welsh? Will they answer a call to arms?"

"How will you find out?" asked the minstrel.

Owain gripped the minstrel's shoulder, turned his face so he was forced to look straight at him, and said, "*You* will find out. You'll cross the channel to England and go on to Wales. Everyone will welcome you because you bring them songs. The English won't mind you being French if you're a minstrel, and the Welsh will treat you as their friend. When you have found beyond any doubt that Owain Lawgoch can return as Owain, Prince of Gwynedd and find a land fit to rule, then you'll come back and tell me. If the answer is good then my French friends will do the rest. and I shall be Prince of Wales indeed. It's time the English felt an invader's sting on their own land."

"And if I say I won't go?" asked the minstrel.

"Then that song of Roland will be the last you'll ever sing."

"I can't speak Welsh," said the minstrel.

"But you can speak English, can't you?"

"I can sing it."

"Then you can speak it. Besides, you're used to new songs. You'll pick up Welsh." *Which is more than you have,* the minstrel thought. "I'll give you food, drink and money to take," Owain continued.

Well, the prospect seemed better than looking for work in his own beleaguered land. He might travel in more style than he was used to.

"You must have a token to prove to my countrymen that you're who you say you are," said Owain. He shouted to a soldier. "Give me the dagger of my ancestor Prince Owain Gwynedd." The solder opened a huge wooden chest and brought out a leather sheath. He gave it to Owain, who handed it to the minstrel. "Look at it," he said.

The minstrel saw the hilt of a dagger chased with strange, intricate carvings and set with precious stones. Owain drew out a shining blade.

"Take it," said Owain. "Spanish steel and Welsh gold. A fine combination, eh? Let it defend you in your journey, because you'll meet many enemies. But a true Welshman seeing it will know you for a friend and messenger. Leave the sheath with me. When you've succeeded in your task, give the dagger back. Only then will it return to this sheath." The minstrel took the bare dagger. "It's yours," cried Owain. "For now." There was a hint of menace in his voice.

The sallow-faced man called James leant across and whispered in the minstrel's ear. "Don't fear Owain," he said. "But never forget: fail in this task and you'll have me to answer to. I am *much* more dangerous."

Suddenly, Owain roared with laughter and clapped the minstrel on the back once again. "Here I am, sending you away on a journey, and I don't even know your name."

"Guillaume," the minstrel replied. "Guillaume de Lay."

2

As Guillaume wonderingly put the magnificent dagger to his belt, Owain spoke again. "It's too dark to travel alone. You might meet robbers." The men roared with laughter. "Stay a night, eat well and leave in comfort. My scribe will write the letter you'll take. My call to arms."

Soon the letter was done. Owain sealed it with a signet ring. "Written in fine, ringing Welsh," he said. "This seal makes you welcome to true Welshmen and opens any door. Make for the north of the country where my ancestors ruled." He was silent for a moment. Then he said, "There are many Welshmen whose support I need. The most powerful, whose word counts for much, is Gruffydd Fychan of the House of Powys. Find him, gain his trust, and your quest is as good as done."

"Where shall I find him?" asked Guillaume.

"Wales has changed since my father's day and the English have destroyed many great houses. Once the princes of Powys lived at Sycharth, but I'd be very surprised if such a place is still standing. Go north, Guillaume, go north and find out."

Guillaume was given a mattress and furs in which to wrap himself. He slept at once. Next morning, he was filled with more mutton, bacon, fresh eggs, bread and rich milk. Then Owain led him outside. "No messenger of mine goes to Wales on foot," he said. "Take this."

Yet another surprise in this time of strange twists of fortune. A groom led out a horse – no knock-kneed nag but a fine, spirited creature. Guillaume wondered which wealthy man once owned it. "The news you'll bring back is worth a hundred horses," said Owain. "Good luck – and may you meet no one like me on your way. And keep away from the English unless you are singing to them."

As he was mounting the horse, James of the sallow face appeared. "You can't avoid the English," he murmured. He looked round to be sure that nobody watched. Then he slipped another letter into Guillaume's tunic. "To get a ship across the Channel you have to go to Calais. It belongs to King Edward now. Show my letter and they'll let you in without question." His voice dropped to a whisper. "Remember me. My name is Lamb. James Lamb. Hide Owain's letter until you reach Wales. If the English find it, you're dead. Be careful. Now the English are in charge, many Welshmen do very well out of it." He looked up at Guillaume, his mouth twitching with suppressed laughter. "But rather more don't. It's up to you to find out which is which." He smacked the horse on its rump and Guillaume's long journey started.

Nobody stopped him in this land devastated by war and plague. Only now did he think calmly about what he had let himself in for. Why not just disappear, never to be heard of by Owain again? No, he had accepted hospitality, a fine dagger, a horse. He had given his word. He was a man of honour. All Guillaume's instincts told him that Owain was as well. Even though he was a brigand willing to slice anybody's throat for loot, his ambition burned strong and what he said he meant.

James was a worryingly different matter. Owain trusted him completely, yet he had written a letter giving Guillaume safe passage through the strongest English garrison in France. So the English must trust him as well. He had to be false to one or the other. If he was false to Owain, then he was a spy for the English. If he was true to Owain, then the game he played with the English was very different. This letter James had written – it might be a trap. Though for the life of him, Guillaume couldn't see any point in Lamb trapping him.

This James, and his sallow face with its enigmatic smile, made him shiver with a fear to which he could not put a name. He had to trust somebody. But he didn't know who.

Guillaume was not a happy man as his horse took him further away from Owain's tent.

He spent a flea-bitten night in Rouen. He whiled away the time by sewing Owain's letter into his cloak where nobody could find it.

Another day's ride brought him to Calais. Here, his heart nearly failed him. The English had made the town a fortress. Wherever he looked, English soldiers guarded, patrolled or just stared balefully at him. "My life isn't worth a sou," he murmured. Yet his main feeling was boiling anger. How dare the English call Calais their own? How dare such a small but devilish land make fools out of the greatest kingdom in Europe? No Frenchmen could rest until Calais was theirs again.

He reached a town gate. A sentry blocked his way. Guillaume shouted in in an English more suited to music than speech, "Let me through. I bear a letter giving me the right."

"They all say that," grunted the sentry. Even so, he read the letter James had written, then looked at him suspiciously for a long time while Guillaume held his breath. At last the sentry spoke. "Enter," he said gruffly, and Guillaume silently said a prayer of thanks as another soldier brought him down to the harbour.

The ship with its single sail caught a fair wind across the Channel. His first view of the enemy's land was of white cliffs looming up in grey drizzle like a traitor's gate. He disembarked at Dover and set off inland.

Now began his journey in a hostile country. His two letters, one in English, one in Welsh, seemed to weigh him down with danger. He realized that he was now a spy and, if caught, couldn't say who he spied for. He trudged along narrow trackways, and crossed high, bare, chalky hills where sheep grazed short grass: he slept under stars and drank clear, cold water from dew ponds. Then he came to soft green country and felt better.

The journey was peaceful. He was accepted wherever he went and realized he should not be surprised. England was as plague-ridden as France but no foreign armies roamed the land. The danger came from English soldiers unwanted after the Battle of Crécy, who had formed themselves into marauding bands of robbers. He met poor but easy-going people who listened to his ballads as if he were an angel from heaven. They shared their meagre food and gave him rough shelter. To his surprise he found he liked the English – at least, the poor half-starved wretches he mostly met – and he picked up their language as he learned their songs.

At last he saw high hills like a misty, mauve wall in the distance and knew he was close to Wales. He remembered his purpose and his nerve failed him. No, he couldn't enter that country, perhaps even more dangerous than England – at least, not yet. He turned northwards, as Owain had said, parallel with Offa's Dyke.

Now he was in the Welsh Marches, where grey castles kept the Welsh out of England. His horse walked beside wide rivers, over wooded hills, past manors and abbeys. He stopped in great cathedral cities, Hereford, Gloucester, Worcester, and sang to the people, both his own songs and the English songs he had heard on the way, because for Guillaume, it was a case of once heard, never forgotten.

Always he headed north. He passed the hills of Salop and, after a night singing in a tavern and sleeping on soft straw in Leominster, he was approaching Shrewsbury. Offa's Dyke and Wales were very close now: they hung like a pall in his mind.

It was late afternoon. From low clouds, a fine drenching rain fell. The track was narrow with scrubby trees on either side. As the path turned and he could look way down it, Guillaume saw another horseman two hundred paces ahead. This was rare enough for him to think of catching the traveller up, for company. The traveller rode a fine horse and, as Guillaume drew nearer, he recognized the brown habit of a Benedictine monk. The monk must be very sure no robber would dare attack a man of God, especially when his horse towed a small packhorse loaded with panniers. Surely he should have some sort of escort? Guillaume knew how lucky he had been to come through England unscathed.

Even as he thought, the robbers came: four men hiding in the trees ahead, two on each side of the road. Horrified, Guillaume watched. They sprang out with incredible suddenness. Two pulled the monk off, the other two hurried the frightened horses into the trees. One man held the victim down: Guillaume saw a shiny streak as the other stabbed the monk viciously. He heard a shriek, then the man lay still. His attackers melted into the trees.

Guillaume shook with horror. Even Owain's killings had not chilled him as much as this sudden deadly swoop from nowhere. At last, still unwillingly, he got off his horse and led it. All was quiet now: Guillaume had a feeling – or perhaps just a hope – that the robbers were far away already, counting their gains in peace and secret.

He came to the body. What should he do? He couldn't leave the poor fellow here. How far was Shrewsbury? He bent down. The habit was wet with more than rain: blood soaked through it. The knife had torn right to the monk's chest. His face was strong, weatherbeaten, as though he hadn't spent all his life in the cloister. How terrible to meet such a death without warning, even though it was every traveller's risk.

The monk's eyelids fluttered. His arm made a tiny, jerky movement. A faint groan came from his slightly parted lips.

"You're not dead," Guillaume cried aloud. Now he knew exactly what to do. Surely Shrewsbury and its famous abbey wasn't far? He would take this monk to his own abbey. There would be an infirmary and monks skilled in herbs and medicines. If the monk had a chance of life, they would give it.

First, though, he had to lift him to his horse. Even lifting him could kill him. With strength and gentleness, Guillaume somehow heaved him up and faced him forward, like a tired rider sleeping in the saddle. He felt the monk's wrist. There was a faint beat: he was still alive. Slowly and gently, Guillaume led the horse onwards.

They walked for hours. The rain stopped, the clouds cleared and the sun sank fast to the west. A mile to the east was a great tower. He knew it must be the abbey church.

As he led his horse with its precious cargo, he thought of Shrewsbury, the abbey and Offa's Dyke with Wales so close. The time had to cross that border was near. Only now had he picked up enough English to be understood. Many times he thought he had mastered it but then came to another place where it sounded completely different. Now Wales and a language like gibberish had to be faced, for he had given his word.

As he crossed the bridge over the Severn and came to the abbey, he suspected he might need nearly as much help there as the wounded man he bore.

3

At the great Benedictine Abbey of St Peter and St Paul he was kindly received. "Look to the man," he said urgently. "He's dying."

The willing hands of the brothers took the monk off the horse. When they saw his face, they gasped. "It's Occa," cried one.

"Our good friend and brother," cried another.

"Who would do this thing?" asked a third.

Brother Occa was laid on a stretcher and four brothers carried him to the infirmary. Then a monk said to Guillaume, "How did you find Occa like this? You must explain yourself to Abbot Geoffrey."

Abbot Geoffrey listened to Guillaume's account. "You are from Normandy, is that not so?" he said. "I hear a French voice behind your halting English. Why are you in a land with which your country is at war?"

"I am on an errand," said Guillaume.

"An errand? What errand?"

What should he say? Too much and he'd be in the sheriff's hands as a spy. Too little and he'd be in the sheriff's hands for wounding Occa.

"I bring a message to Wales from a Welshman in France," he said.

"Is he a Welshman of consequence?" asked the abbot.

Guillaume saw that the abbot guessed the answer. No one would take such risks for a man of no consequence. "He has claims to make in Wales and England. He wants to know if he is remembered," he said.

"I believe I know which man you mean," Abbot Geoffrey replied. "Who in Wales do you wish to see?"

"A name was mentioned," said Guillaume. "Gruffydd Fychan."

"I see," said Abbot Geoffrey. Guillaume studied his face: there was no clue to show he knew the name. "We're men of God here, but we're men of our own countries as well. We have as many Welsh as English in our community, and I won't stir trouble by asking you more or telling them more. You're welcome as a guest and free to carry on your journey with our blessing. But first you must taste our hospitality. You've saved the life of our dear brother and we at least owe you that."

Abbot Geoffrey meant what he said. Guillaume was treated kindly, fed simple food and housed for the night in the abbey guesthouse. Before Vespers, he spoke to two monks, who told him much.

Yes, Wales was close - a few miles west and across Offa's Dyke. Not far to the north was Chirk

Castle, home of the Earls of March and solid for the king. Guillaume listened, and thought that he should stay clear of Chirk. But the monks said that if he kept west over Offa's Dyke into Wales, he would eventually come to Sycharth, on the hills above Afon Tatan and Llangedwyn.

"Sycharth?" said Guillaume. He knew that name. Then he remembered what Owain had said. Sycharth might be a burnt-out ruin.

Brother Ralph was a big man with a deep voice, with the English of a man from Mercia. Brother Llew, small and dark, was a Welshman.

"Sycharth is a great house," replied Ralph. "A palace, even."

"It's the home of Gruffydd Fychan," said Llew.

Gruffydd Fychan. Guillaume's heart leapt. So soon and so near. Perhaps his quest would be over very quickly.

"In better days, Gruffydd's grandfather was Prince of Powys. Gruffydd's wife is the daughter of Llewellyn ap Owain, whose forbears were once Princes of Deheubarth."

"Not so Welsh as to stop them serving King Edward," said Ralph.

Guillaume's heart sank. They had gone over to the English. A turncoat was the most savage, treacherous enemy of all.

Ralph was still speaking. "Besides, they live too close to Chirk and the Earl of March to want anything but peace."

So it was a wasted journey. All his travail was for nothing.

"Not so," said Llew. "Man may be frail, but he can make up for that frailty by cunning. The worst enemy to the English is the one they think is their friend. I don't believe the sons of princes don't want to be princes themselves. If I were King Edward, I'd trust no Welshman claiming noble birth. Or any other Welshman if it comes to that." He laughed. "I'm one myself. I know."

As the monks chanted the services of Vespers, Guillaume sat at the back in the dark, listening, sure that the next days held great tests in store for which he would need the guiding hand of a God who didn't care about the vain wishes of English, French or Welsh when the fate of a good man was at stake.

He woke next day feeling refreshed. Yesterday's cloud and rain had gone. The sun was high: it was mid-morning and nobody had woken him, even though the monks' day started six hours before. His first thought was for Brother Occa. He pulled on clothes and went to the infirmary. Two monks bent over a cot in which the wounded man lay. His face was pale, but his beard was trim: the monks had shaved him.

"He's sleeping," said the younger monk. "He should live now. But if you hadn't brought him here, he would have died on the road."

"Abbot Geoffrey knew you would come to see Occa before anything else," said the elder. "He wants to talk to you before you go."

Brother Occa opened his eyes. He saw Guillaume. "This is the man who rescued you, Occa," said the younger monk.

Occa reached up and grasped Guillaume's hands. His grip was unexpectedly firm. "I owe you my thanks," he said. "Tell me your name so I can remember you in my prayers."

"Guillaume de Lay. I am a minstrel from France with a message for all Welshmen. I'm on my way to Sycharth, and a man called Gruffydd Fychan."

"Then God speed you, Guillaume de Lay. I say that even though I'm an Englishman, and was a soldier before I became a monk. I fought Welsh, Scots, yes and Frenchmen too, I'm sorry to tell you. I bore no ill-will: I was doing my duty. But I'll never regret the soldier's calling. It's a noble one, especially when you are, as I am now, a soldier for God. That's why you found me on the road alone. Abbot Geoffrey sends me on journeys for the abbey far and wide because I can look after myself." He laughed. "Though after yesterday you may doubt that. On this journey I've lost chalices and jewels belonging to the Church, but one life means much more than all the riches in Christendom, so I will not be blamed."

"Guillaume," said the other monk. "Abbot Geoffrey waits."

"I shall be praying for you, Guillaume," said Occa.

Guillaume crossed the courtyard in the shade of the abbey church, entered the cloisters and found the abbot kneeling in his cell. He waited until Geoffrey finished his prayers, then listened as he spoke.

"Guillaume, you have done this abbey a great service. You saved the life of a dear brother, loved in both abbey and town. Shrewsbury should reward you and so should we. But what can I do? I can't say to the sheriff, 'Here is a Frenchman with a message from a renegade, exiled Welshman, inciting his countrymen to rebel against the English. You must reward him before you hang him.' "

Nothing passed by this wise man with the thin face. "Letting me go on my journey is reward enough," Guillaume murmured.

"If I let you go I break the king's law. I should send you to the justice of the peace for you to tell him how it happened."

"They'd know I was a Frenchman. They'd hang me."

"Very probably. Poor reward again. No. I shall let you leave, and nobody will follow you from this town."

"Thank you," said Guillaume. "That's reward enough. That and your prayers, if you feel you can make them."

"We can give you prayers and much more," said Abbot Geoffrey. He reached to a little alcove in the stone wall, brought out a wooden casket and opened it. Inside were two small bones. Guillaume knew what they were. "Relics of saints," he said.

"Yes," said Geoffrey. "These don't belong to the abbeyc. They are mine. They are relics of a saint worthy of our praise and awe, who wandered far from her own land, like you, who was steadfast in her actions and cruelly martyred for her faith."

Guillaume looked at the tiny objects. "The knuckle joints from two fingers," he said. "Why are you showing me these?"

"Because from now on, one of them is yours," said Abbot Geoffrey. "May you have protection from a saint who watches over you and gives you steadfastness, so that every choice you make will be the right one." He looked keenly at Guillaume. "Yes, the right one, even if it leads to sacrifice and death."

He felt again in the alcove and produced a small leather bag with a drawstring. He put one of the jointed knuckles inside, tightened the drawstring, handed the bag to Guillaume and said, "Take it, with the thanks and blessing of the abbey and Godspeed for the journey ahead."

Guillaume held the bag tight and knelt in front of the abbot, who placed his hands on his head and gave him a blessing. Then he rose to go. But before he left, he asked one question. "The saint whose relic you have given me. Who is she?"

"St Ursula," Abbot Geoffrey replied. "The Blessed St Ursula."

4

Guillaume stepped westwards out of Shrewsbury without hindrance. It was afternoon: the town was about its work and nobody noticed one traveller. He was still uneasy, despite the abbot's kindness and the comforting feel of the little leather bag slung round his neck. Relics like St Ursula's were powerful things. He had been given a reward indeed.

But Ursula's influence did not extend to the weather. The morning's sun was gone. Clouds and cold wind from the west brought sharp flecks of rain. Guillaume thought about what the monks had said. Chirk Castle to the north, where an English earl lived, Sycharth to the west, home to Welsh princes. He sought Owain's true Welshmen, and Sycharth was where he would find them. Or was it? After knowing years of war in France, Guillaume could see that round here there was certainly peace. Perhaps Owain's fears that they were all English together now were true. Then what would Guillaume's life be worth?

By nightfall, rain had set in, he shivered with cold and his stomach rumbled with hunger. He must rest before he crossed Offa's Dyke. He found a deserted barn, wrapped his cloak round his body, burrowed into rotting straw and shivered himself into fitful sleep. In the morning, he set off again, his stomach groaning and his limbs shaking with cold.

The clouds came lower. Owain's horse picked its way hesitantly along a rough track, steeper and steeper into thickening mist. A fine cold drizzle soaked them. Yes, everything people said about these islands was true. They were dark, cold, rainswept and fogbound. No matter how easy-going the English had seemed, he hated their land. And Wales seemed worse. More and more miserable, pierced with cold and wet, he lost all track of time. Would the sun ever show again through this fog? He wondered if Wales had a sun at all.

The track twisted, sometimes level, sometimes downward, always rough. Guillaume hoped they might descend to a broad plain, a river, a town where he would find food and warmth. But no: always the climb started again, until he wondered if Wales was a land completely in the clouds.

Then, suddenly, the fog cleared. They sky was blue, the sun shone down and warmth crept into every limb. Below, to his left, there was the plain and the river lwith a town on its banks that he had so longed for.

But in front of him was something else altogether. He saw earthworks and a moat with a gatehouse and wide drawbridge. Beyond a surround earth wall were houses, an arcade, a hall and a chapel with a belltower and a high white cross. Beyond that again was another mound and on it a second hall, built of massive baulks of timber. Beyond the moat was a deer park: even from here, he caught a flash of reddish hide. He saw orchards, grazing land, fishponds, a dovecote, even a lawn with peacocks strutting. This was a place fit for princes.

Owain's letter seemed suddenly heavy in his cloak. The monks were right. He had come to Sycharth, seat of the one-time princes of Powys, home to Gruffydd Fychain and his wife, daughter of Llewellyn ap Owain. If these people did not welcome him with open arms, then Owain Lawgoch had no chance. He unstitched the letter's hiding place, took it out and put it in a deep pocket inside his cloak.

Guillaume was indeed welcomed. Once inside the great hall he was taken to Gruffydd, his wife and a girl with a beauty which took his breath away. Gruffydd was a large, strong man, dark-haired and olive-skinned as if he came from far away, from lands where the sun shone brighter. Two massive boarhounds, young but fully grown, lay at his feet. His wife was also dark, but small and dainty. The girl was so radiantly lovely that he hardly dared look at her. They sat in heavy, carved oak chairs. The room was hung with tapestries, clean rushes were on the floor and a bright fire burned in a stone-lined fireplace. Gruffydd clapped him on the back when he saw his harp and roared, "Don't think I'm not proud of our Welsh songs. But hearing them night after night can be wearing to the soul. I'd even listen to something English. For God to send us out of the blue a *French* minstrel – why, it's a miracle. What marvellous chance has brought you here?"

"I've come from France with a message," Guillaume answered. He had already unfastened his cloak and taken out Owain's letter.

"For me?" Gruffydd exclaimed in surprise.

"And for all Wales," Guillaume added quickly. He handed it over.

Gruffydd took it and looked at the seal. Guillaume could not mistake the look of surprise, followed by a frown. Then Gruffydd put the letter inside his cloak. "Messages from France can wait," he said. "You'll eat with us tonight, minstrel, and then you'll sing for us."

"Thank you, my lord," said Guillaume.

"But first, you must know who you're singing for," said Gruffydd. "My wife and –", he indicted the young girl, – "my niece and ward, Rhiannon. You must rejoice with us as you sing. My wife is pregnant, and if she bears a son his name will be Owain, a name fit only for heroes. Rhiannon is betrothed to a fine English knight, Sir Edmund Fitzgrace, kinsman to the Earl of March."

When he heard that, Guillaume's heart sank. A man likely to take Owain Lawgoch's side would not marry his niece off to an English noble.

Later, at dinner, he feasted like an honoured guest, though sitting at the long trestles below the top table. As he ate he heard Welsh songs from the minstrels' gallery. Gruffydd might have grown tired of them, but to Guillaume they were wonderful. The harps sounded clearer, more resonant than his. The bardic voices climbed higher over them, sounding almost unearthly, like angels. His neighbour at the table, a dark, swarthy man with a cast to his left eye, listened intently, beating his hand in time on the table and rumbling with approval.

Guillaume was intrigued. He risked speaking in English. "What does it mean?" he whispered.

The man answered in English. "That singer is one of Gruffydd's favourite poets. His name is Y Bergam," he said. "This is what his poem says. *'In France, there's a man of Wales who's spoiling for a fight. He'll bring a whole army over to avenge his noble father.'* "

"Is that really what it means?" cried Guillaume. He was amazed to hear a prophecy about Owain Lawgoch so soon and clear.

"It is," said the man. "And there's many happy to hear it."

But not, it seemed, Gruffydd. When the song was ended, he rose. "Enough of Welsh," he cried. "There's a novelty here tonight. A musician straight from France, from the court of the king himself."

Guillaume trembled slightly at such a lie. He'd have to be good to justify it. Full of a trepidation he didn't normally feel, he walked forward, feeling scores of curious, foreign eyes on him. A servant escorted him up the steps to the minstrels' gallery. Once there, he forgot everything in the joy of singing. He sang the Breton lays he loved so much, songs of heroes like Roland, stories of the fabled lost land of Ys and Melusine the snake-woman. Now he was coming to the end.

His audience had listened, quiet and rapt. Except Gruffydd. In the end, his attention wandered. Perhaps all music, not just Welsh, tired him. He had brought Owain's letter into the hall. Guillaume could see that the temptation to know more about this mysterious message was proving too much. But when Gruffydd opened it and read, he took no pleasure in it. His face was mottled with fury. He hadn't looked pleased at Y Bergam's poem and he was even angrier to see it come to life in front of him.

Guillaume's voice faltered. He wondered what that fury might mean for him. He tried to sing again but his attention wandered. Now he was conscious of his audience, every different face watching him. And two of those many faces suddenly stood out, as if lights shone on them, and he saw both in the sharpest detail.

One was Rhiannon's. It lifted his soul, sent a flood of pure joy through him, followed by a great longing. Never, it seemed to him, had he seen such perfect beauty. Those laughing eyes, that flowing dark brown hair, that body – so lissom, so perfect. She seemed to be smiling only for him. His soul was stirred and his voice faltered again before he recovered and sang once more – even purer, even clearer, just for her.

And then he looked at the other face, also smiling, but in a different way. This smile mocked him, as if he was the butt of some private joke. And it seemed that he was. *James Lamb had left Owain Lawgoch in France and somehow got to Wales before Guillaume.*

His voice faltered again. At first he was angry. What point was there in giving the message to Gruffydd? Then his anger faded. Instead, he was frightened, and the fear spread until his voice froze and he could play no more. James Lamb's presence here boded ill for him. There was good reason to be frightened. The beauty he had seen a moment before swam out of his reach, part of another life which would never be his.

No matter about Gruffydd, everybody else wanted more. Guillaume pulled himself together and sang an old favourite, nothing heroic – *Lai le Freine,* Song of the Ash Tree, that strange ballad from Brittany.

As the story of the separated twins wound on, he suddenly had a clear vision of himself on a day to come, teaching it to a son. His eyes strayed back to that wondrous girl. His heart leapt again. He wasn't mistaken. She was looking right at him, straight in the eye, but when he paused and smiled back she lowered her eyes with an expression which made his heart beat fast again. The shock of seeing James Lamb died. He had to speak to this woman. He didn't care how he managed it or if he were thrown out of Sycharth in disgrace. *Lai le Freine* ended. Gruffydd stood. "Enough singing," he called. "Thank you, minstrel from France. You've pleased us mightily." Then he walked out of the hall and his family followed. James Lamb with the sallow face filed out last.

Or was he last? Another leap of the heart on this extraordinary evening – the lady was standing still, waiting at one end of the top table as guests and servants milled round her.

"*Waiting for me?*" Guillaume exulted to himself. He pushed his way down the narrow stairway from the gallery. He had to speak to her. He reached her and knelt. "My lady," he said, "you know that I am Guillaume from Normandy, a good minstrel, though Gruffydd was wrong to say I'm from a king's court."

"I know," she replied. Her voice sounded like the clear, melodious Welsh harp played by Y Bergam. Guillaume had to pause before he could say any more.

"Lady, the favour you give by speaking to me makes my heart race and my mind reel," he managed at last. "I don't know what to say."

"Say whatever you want to," the lady murmured. "I shall listen."

Guillaume hoped she would not walk away, offended, at his next words. "I'm nothing but a low-born singer and harpist. But to show my admiration of your beauty I would give a gage of courtly love as great knights do, though I'm no knight and have nothing to give as a gage."

The lady extended her hand and touched his. "Stand up, Guillaume. I don't care about knights, nor about gages of love."

"But you're going to marry an English knight," said Guillaume.

"Am I?" she answered.

Why didn't she say "Yes" and show pride in it? Suddenly, Rhiannon's expression changed. Her mouth pursed in an expression of stubborn dislike. *What have I said?* Guillaume wondered. Then he saw she was mouthing words silently at him. He watched, bemused, and then realized what message she was trying to pass. "*I need help.*" He turned. A tall man, richly dressed, with black hair and a short black beard, was glaring at him.

"Minstrel," the man said. He packed as much contempt as Guillaume had ever heard into that one word. "I know you for a common Frenchman. And if I were not a guest here, owing honour to my noble host, I would take you outside, kill you without a thought and leave your body in the dust like a stray dog's."

He pushed Guillaume aside and seized Rhiannon's wrist. "Be careful who you speak to," he snarled and pulled her to the doorway. There, he turned. "I am Sir Edmund Fitzgrace," he said. "Knight, kinsman to earls and, soon, kinsman to princes."

The last Guillaume saw as they left was Rhiannon's despairing face. *There's danger here,* he thought. *I must get away.* Then came another thought, certain as his own name. *And I must take Rhiannon with me.*

There was a loft over the gallery for minstrels to sleep in. As he stood at the foot of the steps, Guillaume felt powerless. James Lamb's presence here and Edmund Fitzgrace dragging Rhiannon away showed how much he had strayed into matters beyond him.

He climbed the steps to the minstrels' loft and found soft, dry straw to lie on. Y Bergam was curled up in a corner, snoring already. Guillaume put down his pack and harp, took off the leather bag Abbot Geoffrey had given him and felt St Ursula's knuckle-bone inside. He longed to feel its power and goodness streaming through the leather, but it remained a fragment of ancient, lifeless bone. Perhaps he could have offered it to Rhiannon as a gage of love, for all the good it was doing to him. He wrapped his cloak round himself and started some prayers, but could not concentrate. Suddenly, he did not have to.

A face appeared at the top of the steps. Its owner stood on a lower step. "Are you in here, Guillaume de Lay?" the face said.

Guillaume recognized it, dark and swarthy with a cast to one eye. This was the man who had sat next to him as they ate, who had told him what Y Bergam's song meant.

"I'm here," Guillaume answered.

"My name is Rhys. I bring a message. Gruffydd wants you."

Guillaume followed Rhys down the steps, through the hall where serving men and women were still clearing up the mess of leftover food, and to a great door set in the wall. Rhys spoke in Welsh to the servant waiting outside. He nodded at the answer and knocked on the door. A deep voice sounded from within. Rhys and Guillaume entered together.

Gruffydd sat in his chair holding Owain's letter in front of him. The boarhounds still lay at his feet. But what made Guillaume gasp was James Lamb standing at his shoulder, a broad smile on his sallow face.

"Minstrel," said Gruffydd, "I fear you are an ill-judged messenger."

James Lamb's smile stayed fixed and made Guillaume nervous. "My lord," he answered. "I do not know what you mean."

"Then I'll tell you," Gruffydd answered. "Wales once had many princes - princes of Dyfed, of Powys, of Gwynedd and others. I am descended from the princes of Powys and my dear wife from the princes of Deheubarth. You bring a message from a prince of Gwynedd, asking me to support him in a quest to become princes of all Wales. What am I to say to that? Is Gwynedd better than Powys, that he should take it upon himself to rule me?"

Guillaume surprised himself with the speed of his answer. "Surely it's better to have a true Welshman as your prince, instead of King Edward's son, the Black Prince, who spends all his time living in Gascony ravaging my own people, who's never been to Wales and doesn't speak a word of your language?"

Gruffydd threw back his head and laughed. Guillaume knew exactly what Gruffydd would now say. "So how is this Owain or Yvain or whatever you call him, this great Prince of Gwynedd, any different?"

"But he says he's a true Welshman," Guillaume replied.

"Not any more," said Gruffydd. "True Welshmen stay here and do their best for their people and their land, even if it means being nice to the English. It's from those the real Prince of Wales should come."

Guillaume looked helplessly at James Lamb. His smiling face gave no help. But then he spoke. "My lord, you must admit that this minstrel is loyal to Owain and faithful to the orders he was given. Many great lords would give much for a servant as faithful as he is."

I seem more loyal and faithful than you are, Guillaume thought.

"That's true, James," Gruffydd answered "But he has not answered why Gwynedd should rank above Powys or Dyfed or Deheubarth. Or why I should bow the knee to another man who can't even speak my language, when I must do that already to an English king." He paused. "I'm minded to have my question answered," he continued. "I'll let the minstrel go on his way and give his message to anyone in Wales who cares to listen." He resealed the letter and handed it to Guillaume. "Keep that letter safe. If the people of Wales say they want this Owain Lawgoch as their prince, then I'll help his cause. But I tell you this, minstrel. When you've finished and found that everyone answers you as I have, though perhaps not so politely, you'll find I'll be helping nobody but myself. And the best way to do that is to have a son of my own and christen him Owain. *Then* we may see a true Prince of Wales.

Guillaume longed to say, "How can you trust this man at your side when he was in France, telling Owain I should come here?" But some warning look in James Lamb's eyes, despite his still smiling face, stopped him. It would be a dangerous question, and Guillaume had a feeling he was in quite enough danger without that.

"Leave us now," said Gruffydd. "Sleep soundly, minstrel. Stay a day or two and eat well, but then go on your way. Perhaps you'll sing to us again, when you come back and you know just how right I was."

Guillaume bowed, said, "Thank you, my lord," and left the solar relieved at having got out so easily. Yet his mind raced with disturbing questions as he climbed the steps to the minstrels' loft. He didn't want to stay a day or two, not with James Lamb and Edmund Fitzgrace around. But he could see no way to escape, let alone take Rhiannon with him. Unless there was another twist on this strange night of surprises. Before he had pulled himself up to the floor above he heard footfalls on the steps below and a voice whispering. "Guillaume, come back down. Your night isn't over yet."

5

Rhys stood on the steps once more. "Has Gruffydd summoned me again?" Guillaume asked.

"No," Rhys answered. "You'd better move fast, in case he does. You're in danger. Bring your belongings with you. *Now!*"

Guillaume worked feverishly. He put Owain's letter back in his pocket, picked up the cloak, then his pack, harp and the leather bag containing the relic, and clambered down the steps, turning corners he knew he would never find again. He thought they passed the same place several times, as if Rhys was deliberately confusing him. Then, round a corner where there were no lanterns and the darkness almost choked, Rhys stopped.

"Nobody will be listening here," he said, "not even Lamb."

So Rhys knows James is someone to avoid, thought Guillaume.

"Your message wasn't welcome to Gruffydd, whatever he allows you to do next," said Rhys. "And Fitzgrace would kill you as soon as look at you for daring to speak to Rhiannon. He is a jealous man. I fear for Rhiannon. She deserves better than the fate Gruffydd is making for her. Sadly, he loves her as a father and thinks he's doing right. I know better, and so does everybody else."

"What will you do?" said Guillaume.

"First – I must help you get out of here. Second – no, that would be impossible, I must not even think it – or let you either."

"What are you talking about?"

"Some things are too good for us to have a right to expect them. There's another who would dearly love to go with you."

"You mean Rhiannon?"

"*Don't let that even cross your mind,*" said Rhys.

Guillaume did not answer. The mere thought made him tremble.

"Wait here," said Rhys suddenly and was gone.

Now Guillaume was frightened, alone in a cold, dark place, and fearful someone might steal up and slide a knife between his ribs. He wondered if Rhys had played him an unfathomable trick. He stood, shivering, losing track of time. At last he heard footsteps. His hand closed on Owain's dagger.

"Be calm. It's me." Rhys's voice. "Follow me."

They crept back along the passageway. More steps: a great door which Rhys unlocked and swung open, a rush of night air and the shock of cold drizzle on Guillaume's face.

"Down the steps," Rhys whispered.

Like dark wraiths in the fine rain they stumbled away from the hall, then half-ran, half-walked down the high mound to the chapel. They stood a moment under its walls while Rhys cautiously looked round, then whispered, "Quick," and dashed across open land to a dovecote. Inside, pigeons cooed. There was another noise as well.

"There's a horse here," said Guillaume. Is it mine?"

"Of course," said Rhys. "We're not thieves in Sycharth.

A second horse stood patiently in the drizzling rain. "Whose is that?" Guillaume asked.

"You'll see," said Rhys. "You can't go into these wild Welsh mountains on your own."

"Are you coming with me?"

"No. But you'll need a guide. You'll know who in good time."

There were sudden lights and noise from the hall. Rhys cursed.

"You've betrayed me," cried Guillaume.

"Not so. Stay quiet and be surprised at nothing," hissed Rhys. Then he was gone and Guillaume was left shivering by the dovecote.

How Rhys managed to reach the crowd of angry men without being seen, Guillaume didn't know. The next he saw was Gruffydd's face lit up by a flaring torch and then James's face beside it. "He'll have got away, my lord," Guillaume heard James saying. "He was given too much time after leaving your solar. He'll have made arrangements before."

Guillaume heard Gruffydd grunt and call out, "Rhys!"

"My lord?" The swarthy, bearded man showed in the torchlight.

"What do you know about this?"

"The minstrel said he wanted his horse made ready and left where he could ride away early tomorrow morning."

"And where were you to leave it?"

With a sinking heat, Guillaume waited for Rhys to say, "By the dovecote." But Rhys said no such thing. "He asked that it be led out of the stables and tied up outside where he could find it."

"And you did what he asked?"

"He was our guest, my lord."

"Hospitality has its limits, Rhys," Gruffydd answered. "Is the horse there now?"

"Gone, my lord. Yet the watchmen tell me that nobody has come to the gatehouse and crossed the drawbridge."

"He's escaped somehow," said James. Is he important enough to follow and bring back?"

"It's not for me to say," Gruffydd replied. "He's done me no disservice beyond bringing a message he's not responsible for. And he did sing well. It's Edmund he may have wronged."

Guillaume saw another face in the patch of torchlight. Edmund Fitzgrace. "My lord Gruffydd," he said. "If he's done no harm to you, and if my lady Rhiannon sleeps unharmed in her bed, then the minstrel is a man of no account and we can let him go where he wants."

"Rhiannon is safe, I presume?" said Gruffydd.

"Olwen her maidservant says she sleeps soundly," Rhys answered.

"If it had been otherwise, then I would have had the hounds out and the land scoured for him," said Gruffydd.

"And I would have killed him with my bare hands when we found him, and strung his body up for crows to peck at," said Edmund.

"I know you would, Edmund, and I would have cheered you as you did it," said Gruffydd. "But the man is no threat now, no harm's done and we're tired. Dawn's nearly here and I want my warm bed again."

The last Guillaume saw was Edmund's face looking longingly out into the night, as if murdering a low-born French harpist would make him very happy. Then the crowd dispersed, and all was dark and silent.

The wait for his guide seemed very long. He was sure he would be found still shivering here in the morning, for Edmund Fitzgrace to deal him the miserable death that he had promised. Normandy's sunlit hills and woods showed in his mind like a vision of heaven.

"Guillaume." This place was full of whispers in the dark.

This must be the guide. "I'm here," he whispered back.

"We must be on our way. We'll lead the horses until we're across the moat and clear from Sycharth. I know a shallow crossing-place for us." The voice was still an unrecognizable whisper.

Guillaume saw a dark, formless figure, wrapped in a cloak, leading the other horse. He followed, through an orchard, to the moat. The guide whispered, "Stop here. Watch where I go and follow exactly."

The guide stepped into the moat's waters and Guillaume followed. The moat was shallow here.

Soon they were through and leading the horses up the steep bank, saying nothing. Escape mattered more than speech. Dawn broke. Somewhere above the low cloud that spilled out fine rain, the sun must be rising. Only now did Guillaume look back.

Sycharth was well behind them and no life stirred there yet.

The guide turned and no longer spoke in a whisper. "Now we ride, as fast as we can before the hounds are out and the hunt is up."

For a moment, Guillaume was too shocked to speak. This was a voice he had heard just once, and had thought never to hear again, a dear voice, a wonderful voice. In the strengthening light he looked at the face under the hood because his ears might be playing tricks on him. No, his ears were true, and so were his eyes.

The guide who had brought him out of Sycharth was Rhiannon.

Why had she done this? Rhys had said, and her servant Olwen agreed, that she was asleep in her bed. But that wasn't true. Their meeting must have been the same bolt of lightning for her as it was for him – though Rhys said she was desperate to get out of Fitzgrace's clutches, which meant she might take any help going. He managed a few words. "How long will you be my guide? Will you turn back to Sycharth soon?"

She answered, "You have a journey throughout Wales, I believe. I shall go with you."

Guillaume knew he should thank God, not just for escape from a dangerous place, but for having an impossible dream come true. This wonderful creature had thrown in her lot with him. Or had she?

As they rode, always north-west, always higher, along narrow tracks with bare, short-grassed slopes stretching into mist either side, he went on thinking. He went over the events of the past night again and again, from the moment he had entered Sycharth to his final, secret leaving of it. Nothing seemed quite right; nothing rang true. The refrain which kept hammering through his mind was this: *the things which have happened to me are not what they seem.*

Then the two of them, Rhiannon and Guillaume, were swallowed up in grey mist, vanishing beyond sight into the lonely spaces of Wales.

PART TWO

1369
A Son's Tale

7

July, 1370. Nineteen years had passed since Guillaume and Rhiannon rode away from Sycharth. Joslin de Lay, minstrel from France, now nineteen years old, was close to the end of his quest to Wales. Hereford was far behind and his friend of the last months, the doughty Crispin Thurn, was but a memory. By now Crispin would have married his Eleanor and returned to his newly regained estates.

Joslin sat at the top of a high wooded hill, called the Black Mountain by the people hereabouts. Nearby, his horse Herry munched the short grass. Five miles before, they had scrambled across Offa's Dyke, where true Wales began, and passed through Clun Forest. Now Joslin looked over treetops west and north to see rolling land beyond, dotted with sheep. On the horizon were hints of real mountains.

The day was fine and sunny. This was a land of music and stirring deeds, where wonderful things were possible, a land which contained his life's secret and the key to his future fortunes. He had come through the pitfalls of his journey and now it was nearly over. He fingered the locket he had worn since his father died, shook it and heard a rattle inside. When he found the key to that locket everything would be clear.

Now he was pushing northwards. Some instinct, some submerged memory, kept him on his way. He took his father's dagger from his belt and remembered another voice, Randolf Waygoode, master painter in London, who had kept the dagger safe while he stayed there. Joslin looked at the jewelled, finely-wrought handle set with gems and heard Randolf admiring the craftsmanship. "*Your father must have performed a great service to a nobleman to be given this,*" he had said.

But daggers were not just things of beauty. They killed. With a pang which made tears start, he remembered the moment, almost a year before, when his father had given him the dagger and the locket. Guillaume lay dying on the deck of *The Merchant of Orwell,* bound for England. He had been stabbed in the back in the count's castle at Treauville. Who would murder Guillaume de Lay, minstrel of honour, loved by everyone? An English lord perhaps, one of the embassage at the castle on some unknown errand, as war raged between England and France. Or that one who haunted Joslin's dreams, with sallow, pockmarked face and twisted mouth, staring mockingly down every corridor. It was because of him that Guillaume kept to his room when the English came, and saw nobody except when his duty to the count meant he had to sing.

Now Joslin heard his dying father's voice on *The Merchant of Orwell*'s deck as sailors poled the ship out of harbour to catch winds from the open sea. Guillaume opened his eyes. "*Where are we bound?*"

"*England,*" Joslin replied.

"*Ah, the western ports: Fowey, Plymouth, Brixham. Wherever you land, remember. North for Wales . . .and when you are in Wales, look for the blessed St Ursu- . . .*" His voice failed and his eyes closed. When they opened again he managed weak words. "*My harp is yours. You'll need it. My dagger's yours also. Pray God you'll never need it. And –* " he indicated round his waist a thin belt with the tiny locket on it – "*these are yours too. Wear them always. There is only one key . . . and it belongs to your mother . . . find her . . . and know why this has been.*"

"*I will, Father, I will,*" cried Joslin.

Guillaume spoke no more. He was dead.

So Joslin sailed on – but not to Fowey or Plymouth. This ship was bound for Suffolk on the English east coast. He landed at Ipswich and had a long, dangerous journey across England, taking nearly a year, seeing him nearly married once, and nearly dead far more often. All to search for his mother and the key to open the locket which held such secrets. And with such scanty clues. *Wales. The blessed St Ursu -. . .*

He'd always worn the locket. He hung the thin belt round his neck now and wore a moneybelt round his waist. He took the locket off and looked at it. His mother had the key. Who, where, was his mother?

"*Where is my mother?*" he had often asked when he was young, and back came the reply, "*Your mother is far away, if she is alive at all.*"

He looked down from the Black Mountain across fields of wheat and rolling sheep country, towards the mountains far away. His heart sank. Wales looked very large. He'd never find his mother with the starveling clues he had. When he did find her, she might not want to know him, or he might learn she'd been dead these many years, her bones mouldering where he would never find them.

"*The blessed St Ursu - . . .*" Would that be "Ursula"? Yet Dafydd, a Welshman Joslin had met near Oxford, had said, "*I know of no church with such a name. But a convent – let me see. There are nunneries enough in Wales. But with so little to go on I fear you'll have a long search.*"

He pulled himself together. He hadn't been so downcast in England before, even when death stared him in the face. *Think. Think.*

Slowly, what he had been taught as a child by the priest came back. Ursula lived a thousand years ago. She came from Britain, the daughter of a Christian king. She fled across the sea because she wouldn't marry a pagan prince. She was martyred with her many followers in Cologne, in Germany, because she would neither give up her religion nor marry a new suitor, the chief of the Huns. Later, the bones of a thousand people had been found in a huge grave in Cologne – the remains, everybody said, of Ursula and her followers. They were sent as relics all over Christendom. Any one of the bones might be from St Ursula herself, so they must all be venerated.

Ursula, the saint who met her death because she twice refused to marry men she could not love. Joslin pondered on this. Was that like his own mother? She might have refused to marry Guillaume. If she had, then she rejected her own son, which would mean that after all the danger he'd come through, he'd been on a fool's errand. For an hour he sat feeling empty and depressed, looking over miles of unknown land.

His father must have come to Wales. If only he could follow his path. But that was lost in the past. He must go on, make a path of his own. He stood, took Herry's bridle and led the horse gently down the Black Mountain. And now came a feeling very familiar during this last year.

He was being followed.

Who by?

A chance thief happy to slit a throat for a few coins, perhaps. Or something different?

He looked back over his long journey from his familiar, beloved France to this foreign place in which he was still a stranger. He remembered all the danger, all the terror. But he also thought of those good people from whom he had parted along the way. John Gibbon, the thatcher, wretchedly hanged before his very eyes as he expected the same fate for himself. Robin, dear Robin, foully murdered.

Alys, beautiful Alys, whom he had loved so much and nearly married. Matt and Johanna in Oxford, wise Gervase and even Wat Fisher, murderous scourge of the University, who turned into a stout ally after all. He remembered Miles and his travelling actors in Coventry and little Margery, who braved the devils all alone. And Crispin, brave, inscrutable, steadfast Crispin, with whom he had faced death in many dreadful guises. Now Crispin, like Randall Stone, had come into his own and could marry Eleanor, the apothecary's daughter at last. All gone, never to be met with again but never to be forgotten either.

None of those would be following him. They were concerned with their own lives now. Perhaps, they would never forget him. Maybe they would. Whichever, he would be content.

Except for one. He suddenly recalled that last meeting in the castle in Stovenham.

"Come with us," he urged.

"If it weren't for my father, I would. But I'm loyal too, so I must stay."

Joslin saw there was no persuading her. He took both her hands and they kissed.

"One day I'll come back for you," he said.

"Perhaps, before that, I'll go looking for you," she replied.

They kissed again and as they did so, both wondered if what they had just said could ever possibly come true..

He suddenly longed for her – Gyll, the girl who had rescued him from his condemned cell and guided him to a place of safety. Without her, he would have been hanged on a public gallows. He had loved her then and even when things were at their worst he had never forgotten her. And, he realized, he loved her now as well. And had throughout his journey. But he could never go back to Stovenham. not now, when he might be on the brink of ending his quest.

Then he seemed to hear her voice, right beside him.

'Perhaps, before that. I'll go looking for you.'

How could you? he thought. *What guiding star could possibly lead you east to west to this lonely place in another country?*

No, it could never happen

She is lost to me along with all the others,

But someone *was* looking for him. Every instinct which the last year had honed so sharply told him so - and also said that seeker was close by and meant him harm.

As soon as Joslin turned, the man dodged behind a tree. He smiled to himself as he watched Joslin and Herry continue downwards. Then he whispered, "*So close now, Joslin. What started before you were born is nearly done, one way or the other. Yes, you could be a fitting foe for me and perhaps a staunch friend as well. I've seen enough these last months to show me you're capable of both. Perhaps even more.*"

Then, whether to hide his features from Joslin or from the whole world, he passed his cloak over his sallow, pockmarked face and twisted mouth and followed them down.

Joslin led Herry away. Once out of the trees, he rode again.

The ground fell towards a river valley. The day's end was near. Where there were rivers there were towns, people, houses, taverns, places to rest in and perhaps earn money. He rode on for an hour until he saw a small town ahead, perhaps a mile away, a church with a tower and a wide river beyond. He was about to spur Herry on, then hesitated. He could see a motte, a mound with a stone keep and watchtower on the top. That meant English soldiers were here – and he steered clear of them, because a year before it was English soldiers, under the orders of their earl, who had nearly had him hanged.

As he paused, he heard hoofbeats. A galloping horse was catching him up. His heart lurched with fear. He was still being followed. His hand closed on the hilt of his dagger. Then shock joined fear as he recognized the rider.

His mind took him back a year and he saw again an image which had hardly left him since. The Count of Treauville's castle. A sallow, pockmarked face with a twisted mouth, silently laughing, mocking, jeering, from the ends of corridors. His father frightened in a way Joslin had never seen - and then dying on the deck of a ship bound for England.

And now the owner of that face was rapidly drawing close.

Joslin's first instinct was to gallop away. But he had come to Wales to find the answers to questions. Of all the people he had met, this man might have them. Providence had brought him to this moment, and it must not be shirked. His heart beating fast, he waited.

"So, Joslin de Lay. I can speak to you at last."

Yes, that face would disturb anyone's sleep. "Why should you want to speak to me?" he answered.

"Why not? I've tracked you all this way, watched your exploits and come to admire you. You're not to be taken lightly, so I'll never make that mistake."

"Exploits? What do you mean, exploits?"

"You know what I mean. All those miles away in Suffolk, you set a village by the heels and faced down an earl and his family. Then you came to London, found a murderer, nearly married a lovely girl and almost died of the plague. In Oxford you might have had your heart ripped out and –"

"How do you know what happened in Oxford?"

"Joslin, your time has been full of adventures and I've seen them all. But this part of your journey really counts for something, and matters to me just as much as to you. We're together in Wales, where all the secrets will be laid bare."

"Why does it matter? Why were you in the castle in France? What were you to my father?"

"Your father? Oh, you mean Guillaume. He had good cause to be frightened of me."

Joslin considered the situation. He would love to ask: "Did you kill my father?" But what if the answer came back, "Yes, and now I'll kill you"? Something about this man said that he might. "Who *are* you?" Joslin asked. He might know the name: perhaps Guillaume had mentioned it.

"Don't worry about who I am. You're going to need me now. I've no doubt you're hoping for a well-deserved sleep in that town ahead."

"Why shouldn't I have one?"

"The Welsh call that town Y Drenewydd. The English call it Newtown, because that's what it is. A little piece of England, set down for the English to make sure that Edward's rule holds in a land whose native people long to have him out of it. The English have even built a castle to stop trouble. You've been welcomed in English towns in England, but I wouldn't be so sure about an English town in Wales. For years there've been rumours of a Welsh prince bringing an army from France to make the folk rise in rebellion, and that will be the end of the English here. If the English find you're French, who knows what they might do? It's not hard to know you're French, is it?" For some reason, that last remark struck him as funny and he laughed disturbingly. "So, if you're to spend a peaceful night in Newtown, you'll need protection. Who better than me to make sure you have it? You've no idea how many people feel safer in their beds if they know I'm nearby to look after them."

The man smiled at some hidden joke. Joslin wasn't frightened now. He was angry. He was being laughed at.

"I'm tired of this," he said. "Either you tell me who you are, what you want with me and why you were in the count's castle last year, or you leave me alone to find the truth myself."

"It's not so easy," said the man. "You'll never find the truth on your own. You came here knowing nothing and now, after almost a year, you still know nothing. If you did, you wouldn't be in this part of Wales."

"I know where I'm going," said Joslin stubbornly.

"Joslin, should I laugh or cry? It's obvious that you don't. Do you know who you're looking for?"

Joslin was silent.

"Did Guillaume tell you your mother's name?"

Silence again.

"Strange. But he told you why he was in Wales years ago?"

Still silence.

"If you know neither of those things, then you won't get very far."

"I'll get where I want to be in my own time."

"Then you need to know what questions to ask and who to ask them of. You must hope that not too much happened in the last nineteen years to wipe away all trace of everything you seek. People talk about finding needles in haystacks. Your task is like finding a needle somewhere in all the hay in Wales. Let me be your guide, Joslin. Together we can find the truth."

"Never," said Joslin. But there was one bit of truth he was certain about. "I do know something, and you can't deny it," he said.

The man smiled. "And what might that be?"

"*You killed my father.*"

The man shook his head sorrowfully. "Oh, Joslin, that just shows how ignorant you are, and how shameful it is that you've been kept so all these years. I never killed your father. I couldn't kill your father."

"Why not?"

"I *am* your father."

8

"No!" Joslin screamed. *"I won't listen!"* He pulled Herry round, dug his heels into the horse's flanks and made him go.

The man shouted, "Come back, Joslin. As father and son we have so much to talk about." But after a mile, when Joslin looked back, the road was empty. The man must have gone on to Newtown.

What a monstrous lie. *Guillaume* was his father. *Guillaume* alone had passed on his talent and made him into a minstrel.

Joslin was near the river. There was so much land to search. If he sought a needle, it would have to shine very bright to be seen. He longed for a helper to encourage him, solace him. But he must search alone.

He came the edge of the river, dismounted, tethered Herry to a tree branch and sat down by the water to think. The soft sound of flowing water calmed his mind but saddened his spirit and deepened his unhappiness until it became a black pit of despair.

His quest was over. This man had taken away all meaning to his life. The hope that had sustained him for nearly a year was snuffed out. All was pinytless. He took out his dagger, fingered the blade and for one desperate moment he . . .

No, not that.

Suddenly, the shock of what he had so nearly done brought him back to sanity like a coracle righting itself in a stormy sea and he was restored to thoughts he had before that disastrous revelation.

But it seemed so long now since that sweet memory of Gyll, *"Perhaps, before that, I'll go looking for you"*, and the fleeting joy it gave him before reality stepped in again. j

He had no idea how long he stayed motionless in his black trance. But at last he roused himself. Yes, he had to finish his quest, for better or for ill. He stood up, untethered Herry, remounted and looked round him as if he were seeing everything for the first time. Things were different now. He refused to believe his quest was over. He had to be single-minded. No more distractions. No more thoughts of wshat might have been and what might yet be.

And yet the little voice still said, *"Perhaps, before that, I'll go looking for you."*

With a deliberate effort he shook it off, resolving never to think of it again. A strange feeling that he had cast away a pearl of great price took its place.

Dusk was near. Ahead, a thick wood stretched from the river and up the valley. A trackway came over the top of the valley and disappeared down into the trees. It was a wide, well-used path, which passed through the wood and made a ford across the river.

Should he shelter for the night in the wood? The trees stretched in front, lining the bank, climbing up the valley side, dark, silent, forbidding. He shivered. Forests like this – he hated them.

As he hesitated, he sensed something strange. The evening was still, yet the treetops were moving. Why? What, or who, was hidden in them? He was certain there was danger in those trees, real, death-dealing danger. Robbers who would kill were lying in wait. He was sure of it. What should he do? If he went back he'd meet his scourge again. Nor would he gallop for the ford. Once he was in the trees the robbers could pick him off like boys killing crows with catapults. He would turn Herry off the road, so they climbed the bank and round the top of the trees to regain the riverside track beyond. There would be other ways to cross the river. He pulled Herry round and started the laborious climb up the lonely hill.

Or was it so lonely? Something was coming along the track down the hill, making for the trees and the ford. A horseman with a banner, and soldiers marching, escorting a four-wheeled covered wagon pulled by three horses. Someone important, needing protection, was inside. The procession moved slowly. There were eight soldiers, four on each side of the wagon. The leader's horse was caparisoned, like a knight's.

Now Joslin was sure he was right about robbers in the wood. This cart and its escort must have been seen lumbering through Wales for a long time. Perhaps word had passed along the road quicker than they travelled. There might be rich pickings on board. So the thieves were waiting for the party to run into their ambush.

He must stop them. He spurred Herry on. *"Wait!"* he cried. He ran to the leader, dressed in half-armour and chain-mail. The banner he carried hung limply in the still air.

"Be careful," Joslin called. "There's danger waiting in the trees."

"How do you know?" said the leader. "Are you part of it?"

"No. But I think there are thieves lying in waiting to ambush you."

Then the leader said something which made Joslin rock back in his saddle in amazement. "I know you. I've seen your face."

The other solders slowed and the wagon driver reined his horses in. "If the man says there's danger, there's danger," he said.

"How do you know me?" said Joslin.

The leader ignored him. He took out his sword and pointed forward. "We go on," he shouted.

"Then, even if you don't believe me, be careful," Joslin cried.

The nearest soldier turned to him. "Don't you worry, young lad," he said. "If *he* won't be careful, you can be sure we will." The procession continued down the hill.

Then, in a sudden moment, a gift from Providence, a dizzying reversal, Joslin's life turned on its axis again for the second time that day.

The wind freshened. A breathy gust made the banner stream out. It was divided into quarters. In each quarter was a different creature: fox, hare, otter, eel. How he knew that banner. The de Noville banner, the banner of the Earl of Stovenham, the first danger he had met in England. Why was it here? As the wagon disappeared, a face appeared from inside the covers of the wagon and looked straight at him. His heart turned over. He didn't dare think the name of the person who was looking at him. He *must* be dreaming. *It was impossible.*

But this didn't feel like a dream. The wind really blew on his face. Herry really sweated beneath him: the man who walked through his nightmares for a year really had turned his life askew that evening. Well, if one thunderbolt had struck, why not another straight after?

The last escorting soldier disappeared into the wood. Joslin knew what he must do. He dug his heels into Herry's sides and, at a gallop, they followed. The change to dark as the branches closed over them was like a candle being blown out. Joslin felt for Guillaume's dagger and prayed he would not have to use it. He saw a flash of bright metal ahead: swords were unsheathed. The soldiers were ready.

They moved deeper into the wood. Joslin kept his eyes on the branches above. How would the ambush come? If bowmen waited, the travellers had no chance. But if the robbers had swords, then perhaps . . .

Suddenly, the thieves were on them. With a great roaring and screaming they leapt out of the undergrowth and down from the trees, and the fight was on. Joslin made Herry stand still, though he felt the horse's fear and had to pull at the reins to stop him bolting. There must be fifteen thieves altogether.

The soldiers ranged round the wagon as the thieves fell on them. In the confusion, above the shouts and screams, Joslin heard something unexpected – a high voice, a woman's voice from inside the wagon. "*I absolve you from my service. Take your chance and go to your minstrel with my blessing.*" Then he saw that the escort leader was not fighting the thieves: his duty was to those in the wagon. He had pulled someone out: there was a blurred sight of him on his horse with a figure clinging on behind, galloping through the trees. He hoped they would find safety.

But he knew that whoever had been rescued was not the one who had looked out at him. The thieves had unhitched the three horses, but four thieves were down and the soldiers were getting the mastery. Joslin rode to the back of the cart, reached in with his right hand as his left held the dagger and cried, "Take my hand."

A small hand caught his. He grasped it and pulled the slight figure out of the wagon. "Get on the horse and cling hard," he cried.

He turned Herry round. He felt a light body behind him. Slower now, the horse strained his way upwards. Outside the trees, Joslin turned him left, round the wood and down to the river. The others would go to safety in English Newtown.

What if this was an illusion, and the passenger wasn't who that fleeting glance had told him it was? He rode on along the river. He felt arms round his waist and hands clinging and did not dare believe they belonged to the one he so much hoped for. Nor did he dare snatch a glance over his shoulder in case whoever it was vanished, as Eurydice disappeared from Orpheus. He almost thought he must be living in a ballad, but if he was, he hoped desperately that he was Sir Orfeo and it was Heurodys who clung to him from behind. After a mile he saw cottages and a church. They drew level to a man driving three sheep. "What place is this, friend?" Joslin asked.

The man looked blankly at him. Joslin tried asking in French. Still blank. Joslin steadfastly maintained his patience because he knew that petulance might destroy the spell he was under. The man must only speak Welsh. Joslin tried the language of another western Celtic land, Brittany. Pointing to the church, he asked in Breton very slowly, and the man concentrated hard. Suddenly he smiled broadly, also pointed at the church and cottages and said, "Abermule." Then he drove his sheep on their way, whistling.

In Abermule they found a tavern with stabling for Herry. Only then did he dare to look at this girl and speak her name. "Gyll?" he said.

"Joslin," she answered.

And then tears flowed at the miracle that had happened.

9

Joslin looked amazed at Gyll's elfin face and wide grey eyes. So many memories came. Wales was indeed a place where miracles could happen.

"How can it be you?" he said at last. "I know I'm dreaming."

"If you're dreaming, so am I," Gyll replied.

"I thought I was dreaming last year in the castle, when you helped me escape the night before they were going to hang me," he said. "I've seen you in dreams since. Why shouldn't this be another dream?"

"It's not," said Gyll.

"How have you come here?"

"Do you remember when you left Stovenham?" asked Gyll.

"Yes. I said that one day I would come back for you."

"And I said that perhaps I'd go looking for you."

"I was thinking about that hardly an hour ago," said Joslin. "I was wishing desperately that you might.

But what guiding star could bring you to this faraway place."

"No, Joslin," Gyll answered. "That's not why I'm here. I was not looking for you. Do you remember how things were in the castle?"

"How could I forget? The earl's elder nephew Stephen was dead, and Francis, the younger, was the new heir. The earl had killed his son Geoffrey with his own hands."

"Yes. And my father the jailer was a broken man, and I resolved to spend my life looking after him until he died. Well, he died not three months later. I don't think he wanted to go on living."

"I'm sorry. He was a good man. He did his best for me."

"I thought some soldier or cook would marry me. I couldn't say no, or how would I live? Then my Lady Isobel helped me."

"Isobel?"

"Stephen's widow. She should have been countess one day."

"I never knew her name."

"Her husband had been murdered," said Gyll. "Francis was in charge now. Roger, the old earl, had gone to a monastery to do penance for killing his son. Isobel felt there was no place for her. She'd never marry again. She would enter a nunnery. And not just any nunnery. To forget old troubles, she would go far away, to one she knew of in Wales. She asked me to be her serving maid and go with her. We'd be two nuns together."

"And you said yes," said Joslin.

"Of course. Stovenham had become a trial to me. And Wales – perhaps, I thought, I would hear news of you. Francis gave us a wagon and horses, a driver and an escort led by a trusted squire, and we made our way through England and into Wales with nobody to hinder us."

"Until you came here," said Joslin.

"Yes. When I heard a voice warning about robbers and realized it was *your* voice, I thought *I* was dreaming. I turned to my Lady Isobel and said, 'That's my Joslin.' She looked at me and said, 'The minstrel? How strange God's ways are.' Then the thieves were on us. We heard shouts and swords clashing and the young squire reached into the wagon and hauled Isobel out. '*I absolve you from my service,*' she cried to me.

"I heard her," said Joslin.

"But she said more," Gyll continued. "'*Take your chance and go to your minstrel with my blessing.*' I thought she spoke nonsense and my last hour had come. Then I saw you close to the wagon, and I knew you'd pull me out, and that I could have an easy conscience because the Lady Isobel whom I served had told me so."

Joslin looked at her and said, "Our ways have crossed twice. Each time we've saved the other from death. I've often felt Providence at my side these last months, but never so much as now. My quest is everything to me. But perhaps this is what I really crossed the sea for." He started a question. "Gyll, will you - ?"

Gyll interrupted him. "I've spent the last months wondering about you, sometimes seeing you in my mind with your mother and married to a Welsh girl, perhaps back in France, sometimes cruelly dead. It was torture to me that I might never know. You must tell me everything that's happened and how things are with you."

"Gladly," Joslin replied. But first he asked for food and drink, and the landlord found them Welsh mutton, rough bread and small beer, and a straw-filled loft to sleep in. When they had eaten and climbed to the loft, they sat down and Joslin told Gyll all his adventures, from when he had left her at the castle until the moment he had pulled her from the cart. When he came to the meeting with the man who had followed him so long and told him something so cruel, he could hardly continue and when she saw his distress Gyll cried with him.

Then he collected his wits and asked his delayed question. "Gyll, will you help me to find my mother and Guillaume's murderer?"

"Of course I will," she answered. "For your quest is my quest."

"Gyll," said Joslin. "You *were* looking for me. and I *was* looking for you, though neither of us realised it. But thinking so clearly of you and longing for you so much when you were so close was not Providence. We did this ourselves. Together, our longings were so strong that we *made* it happen because that's what we wanted most in the whole world. And the world decided that it had to come true."

"I know," said Gyll. Then she lay down and sank at once into a deep, deep sleep.

Joslin watched her. Then, as the tension of a day which had first dealt him the most grievous blow he could imagine and then had lifted him to the highest ecstasy he could comprehend finally ebbed away, he slept too.

Next morning, Joslin's first thought was that they needed another horse. He asked the landlord whether anyone would sell him a strong Welsh pony, saddle and bridle. The landlord knew the very man, and before midday they owned a strong, tough little animal which Gyll rode at once, her face glowing with happiness.

"I must name him," she said. "What is your horse called, Joslin?"

"Herry, after a good friend who died when he shouldn't have done. If I hadn't gone to London he would still be alive."

"A horse is a good memorial," said Gyll. "I shall call mine Gib, after John Gibbon, the thatcher who was locked up in the cell with you and then was hanged. You'd have followed him if you hadn't escaped."

"Escaped because of you," said Joslin. "John Gibbon the thatcher. I often think about him. Gib is a good name."

They left Abermule and crossed the river over a rickety wooden bridge. The weather stayed fine. They headed north-westwards again, following a stream tumbling fast into the river. Steep woods stretched away on either side. "Where are we heading for?" asked Gyll.

"I don't know. There's only one man to ask, the man I met yesterday and fled from. I know he killed my father in France. Now he's followed me across England."

"But didn't you tell me that this man says *he's* your father?"

Joslin's mouth pursed with anger. "He's not my father. Guillaume is. I lived with Guillaume all my life. He taught me all I know."

"But, for a ward, a guardian can be as good as a parent. You never knew your mother. You never knew about Wales until Guillaume was dying. Why didn't he tell you before?"

Joslin rode on silently. He had to think about this, and the more he thought, the more his heart sank. "You're right," he said. "There's only one person who knows the truth. We have to find my mother."

"Where shall we start?" Gyll asked.

"I don't know," Joslin replied. "All I have is a locket that only my mother has a key for, and something about the blessed St Ursula."

"Let me see the locket," said Gyll.

He took it from his neck and gave it to her. She picked at the keyhole with her forefinger, then shook it. Again the rattle.

"What can it be?" she said. "Is there a church of St Ursula here, or a nunnery?"

"I don't know. Were you going to a nunnery called St Ursula's?"

"No," she replied. "Why are you so sure it's in north Wales? Did Guillaume tell you?"

"No. I just feel in my bones that it is. Before he died, Guillaume said, 'North for Wales.' But that means nothing. Even south Wales is north of Devon or Cornwall where he thought I would land. Dafydd in the Henley tavern said go north as well, but that was because there were nunneries in the Marches which might be dedicated to St Ursula. He was only trying to be helpful."

"Perhaps there was something else Guillaume said, years ago. You've forgotten it, but it's there, deep in your mind."

"Perhaps," Joslin answered. "I just feel that I'm right."

The path kept straight, but now the stream bubbled towards them from their right, down the slope. They passed it and kept on up the valley. Then Joslin stopped. "Look ahead," he said.

It was a familiar sight. A ridge with a stone wall on top of it and beyond it the great tower of a castle keep. Where there was a castle, there was trouble.

They turned off the path into trees to get out of its sight. "There'll be soldiers," said Joslin. Then he looked at Gyll, very seriously. "You know that now you're with me you're a fugitive. Especially in Wales. To an English knight, a Frenchman in Wales means treachery."

"I know," Gyll replied. "It doesn't matter. It's you I'm with, not a French spy. I'm with a man who's looking for his father's murderer."

Joslin felt a surge of gratitude. "So you do believe I'm Guillaume's son," he cried. "I thought you didn't."

"I shall always believe it," said Gyll. "Whatever that man says. How could I not?""

10

The path was difficult: often they had to dismount and lead the horses. By mid-afternoon, when they had only managed five miles, Joslin had that familiar feeling of being followed. At the top of a hill, he turned round, pointed and said, "Look." Far behind was a man leading a horse.

"It's him," he said. "He won't give up now. He follows, but he doesn't catch up. He could, I'm sure. Why doesn't he?"

"I don't know," Gyll answered. "We'll just go on."

So they did, and every time they looked back, there he was, no nearer, no further behind, but keeping them in his sight, mile after mile.

They came to a wider, well-used path, almost a road, which kept to the lower slopes between the hills, and they rode their horses again.

"We'll gallop," said Joslin. "We'll get away, we'll leave him behind."

Gyll looked back. "His horse can gallop faster than my little pony," she said. "If he wants to catch us he'll do it."

As evening approached the man still followed, as if they were tied together by a long rope. Clouds formed and a sharp wind blew. The sun disappeared. They came to a little knot of wooden, turf-roofed cottages clustered round a tiny church. The only sign of life was an old woman cutting the tops off turnips. Joslin used his method of the night before to find out where they were. Once again, the woman found something to recognise in his Breton and told him, "Tregynon". Before he could ask if they could get food and shelter, Gyll nudged him. He turned to see their dogged hunter leading his horse towards them.

"We must go," Joslin cried.

"Too late," she answered.

The man spoke in Welsh to the old woman. Once or twice, he pointed to Joslin and Gyll and the woman looked at them and smiled. Then she left her turnips, put her arms round Gyll, cried out delightedly and pulled Joslin into the same embrace. A smile split the man's pockmarked face – his twisted mouth looked grotesque.

"Don't be surprised," he said. "I know this land and its language. I told my new friend cutting turnips that I was accompanying my son and his bride-to-be to the great inheritance and wonderful life which awaited them. I said I didn't mind for myself, but could she find you lodging and food for the night and stabling for your horses. And she can." His smile broadened. "I hope you like turnips."

"I'm not your son," said Joslin.

"But I say you are, and now you're not sure, are you? I know you won't deny that this girl is your bride-to-be." Joslin stayed stony-faced.

"I thought not," said the man. "Now I'll leave you in peace, as young lovers should be left. I've other fish to fry."

He swung himself back on to the saddle. Before he rode off, Joslin said, "Wait a minute. How did you know where to follow us?"

He leant down from his saddle. "Joslin, I don't believe Guillaume told you nothing. You know where you're going. I heard what happened to Lady Isobel last night." He looked at Gyll, the same smile playing round his lips. "I heard how she absolved you from her service and how the minstrel rescued you. I thought you'd most likely find shelter in Abermule and then head north-west. I rode after you on the opposite bank and craved admittance to Dolforwyn Castle, close to Abermule. And there I met a friend, and we watched from the walls until we saw you go by. Then I knew that what I thought was true."

He laughed. "When you reach your destination you'll get a nasty shock. You'll find proof that I'm right and you won't be able to deny it." Then he pulled his horse round and rode back the way he had come, into the growing, empty darkness.

Gyll watched him go. "You know I don't believe that man's your father," she said. "But I don't think he's deliberately lying. He really thinks you're his son. He says you'll find proof. How can that be, Joslin?"

Joslin had no answer.

The old lady gave them more than turnips - rough, lumpy bread, and weak beer. At nightfall, a few men came home to Tregynon, leaving their sheep on the hills. The old woman and her shepherd husband slept round the dying fire on the earth floor, wrapped in old fleeces. They found fleeces for Joslin and Gyll, who slept soundly. Even so, Joslin was thankful when dawn came and everyone got up.

They were on their way at sunrise, though there was no sun to see. Steady, drenching rain fell from dark clouds. They wrapped themselves in their cloaks but nothing stopped the wet and cold from seeping through. Neither spoke for some time. Then Gyll said, "He must think Guillaume told you where to go and how to get there."

"It's clear that he knows where," said Joslin. "What does he mean about finding proof he's my father when we get there? That worries me, Gyll. I think he'll always be a step ahead of us."

"We need to know what concerns him most," Gyll replied. "Is it you, Guillaume or your mother?"

"We have to find out about St Ursula," said Joslin. "She's the key to everything. We must find a priest and ask him. This road has to lead to somewhere bigger than Tregynon. We'll just have to keep going and never mind the rain."

That evening, wet through and shivering, they found the bigger place they craved - Llanfair Caereinion, a small, well-set-up town with a church and an inn. They found stabling for Herry and Gib at the inn and a good fire to dry themselves beside and get their blood flowing again, with food better than the bread and turnips of Tregynon. Then they asked the landlord whether there was a church of St Ursula nearby.

"No such," he said. "But as for further afield, I couldn't say. You must ask the priest."

"Where will we find him?" asked Joslin.

"Why, saying mass in the church," was the answer.

They found him in his church. "As for St Ursula," he said, "I know no church, no, nor monastery or nunnery in the whole of Wales. And yet . . ."

"Yes?" said Joslin.

"St Ursula is not a Welsh saint. Yet it beats in my mind that I know the name to be connected with something in Wales. Nothing big, nothing important, nothing to tell my flock about, but there all the same, somewhere at the back of my mind. Let me think." They waited. Then he said, "No, it won't come. But I'll tell you who'll know. The monks of Strata Marcella, a great monastery, half a day's ride away. Go east, along the Afon Banwy, and then, when that river bends to your left, follow the valley to your right to Trallwng, which the English call Welshpool. Then turn north again along the road towards Oswestry, and soon you will be in the monastery lands. You can't miss the great abbey itself, close to Offa's Dyke. Yes, if I wanted to know about St Ursula in Wales, the monks of Strata Marcella are the people I would ask."

They left him and came back to the inn. "Tomorrow we go there," said Joslin. "Back to Offa's Dyke."

"We'll be going east again. Our hunter won't expect that," said Gyll.

Joslin felt pleased. "We've done a good day's work. Who knows what the monks at Strata Marcella might tell us?"

Back in the tavern they ate a good supper. When they had finished, Gyll said, "I can't understand why you don't remember anything that happened before you came to the castle in France."

"There's nothing to remember. I was in France all my life," he replied.

"How long was Guillaume there before you remember anything?"

"I don't know. He never said. I just assumed it had been always."

"Then why go to Wales to find your mother? Either she was in France and went back to Wales or you were born in Wales. If you were, then you went back to France. Yet you know nothing about it."

"I must have been too small to know."

"But your mother was never with you. Did Guillaume bring you on his own? Or did she come to France and then go back?"

"Sometimes I thought she was dead," Joslin replied.

"But surely you asked?"

"Of course I did. Guillaume never said more than 'Your mother is far away, if she's alive at all.' Nothing more."

"I don't believe in *nothing*," said Gyll.

That night, Joslin's mind swirled with sights, sounds and feelings which seemed to have meanings – yet when he tried to catch them they vanished. He heard a night watchman call out in Welsh five times, once every hour, before he drifted into uneasy sleep.

When he woke in the morning he felt happy again. They had a destination to reach, and something to find out which might, just might, be the clue to keep them going. This day could bring forth great things.

11

Overnight, the rain stopped. The day was cool and windy, with clouds scudding across a pale blue sky. Joslin was happy as they rode along the river bank. Even though he was almost going back the way he had come, this journey might have a helpful outcome. They made good pace. The slopes were gentler now, the grass greener and more lush. When the sun was high they came to Welshpool. They asked the way to Oswestry and were directed to a road where horsemen and loaded carts passed frequently and the land round about was fertile.

When they saw the abbey church in the distance they reined the horses in and tied them to a tree. Joslin sat down on the thick grass. After a moment he lay back and Gyll lay beside him. The sun was bright now. He closed his eyes and let its light filter through his eyelids. Gyll's questioning began again. "There must be a reason why you're sure you're right to come north," she said.

"Guillaume *said* north, and north seems right to me," Joslin replied.

"There must be more than that. I believe there are memories locked away in that head of yours. Think, Joslin. Think. Think."

He opened his eyes and saw her face very close and her big grey eyes watching him steadily. He was fascinated by those eyes: he loved them and they held him: he looked deep into them as if he saw into the depths of the sea, where he could plunge and sink, and sink again, further, further . . .

He felt powerless. He drifted, further and further away, out of his body, away from this time and place. He let himself go. Now he felt small, cold, wet, frightened. It was dark: there was no sunlight, but a damp, fetid, salt smell. He heard wind blowing, the crash of water, men shouting and loud creaking and straining. Nothing stayed still: he was hurled from side to side, up and down until he thought his stomach would be torn out of his body. But then a strong arm encircled him: a voice he knew and loved said, "Be still, Joslin. You're safe."

He sat up. Puzzled, he turned to Gyll. "I've had a dream. Yet it seemed as real as being under this tree," he said. "I was very small. I was on a boat. Someone I loved was there. It could have been Guillaume. Gyll, what happened to me?"

"You thought and thought," she answered. "Then you fell asleep and remembered what it was like when you were a tiny child."

"I *was* on a boat," he said wonderingly. "Where was I going to? Who was with me?"

Then he looked at Gyll. "Those eyes of yours," he said. "You took me there with them. It was real. I must have been on a boat when I was tiny. Perhaps it took me from Wales to France I wish I could go back there." He fixed his gaze on her eyes again. "Look at me like you did before. Take me back, please."

But this time nothing happened except that tiredness took him. Within a moment he was sleeping soundly while Gyll sat over him, watching and smiling slightly to herself. If he could do this again, and remember more next time, perhaps some of their troubles might be over.

When Joslin woke, the sun was low in the sky. "You've slept half the day away," said Gyll. "It's time to go to the abbey."

They came to the gatehouse and a monk in a white habit with a dark brown apron let them in.

"Cistercians," Joslin whispered to Gyll. "The white monks." To the monk he said, "We're two travellers and we beg shelter for the night."

He wondered whether they would allow Gyll in the monastery. He needn't have worried. "Let me take you both to the guesthouse," said the monk. "One of the brothers will see to your horses."

The guesthouse in the outer courtyard was clean and simple but they would have the most comfortable beds either had slept on for a long time. Sweet-smelling rushes lined the floor and water jugs and basins were by each bed. Gyll was shown into a separate chamber.

"We will eat after the next prayers, when the bell strikes in the early evening for the hour of Vespers," said the monk.

Joslin thought they might as well start their enquiries now. "Do you know of a church in Wales dedicated to St Ursula?" he asked. "Or a monastery, or a nunnery?"

The monk was silent for some time, until he replied, "No, my son. Nothing comes to mind. The one to ask is Brother Jerome. He is our librarian and knows many things in the world better than we do."

The brother who had taken the horses came back to say they were stabled and fed. The first monk asked him to take Joslin and Gyll to the library. Soon they were standing in the half-light amid the parchment volumes. Brother Jerome, as promised, was there, and they asked their question. He, too, thought for a long time. Then he said, "I know of no church, no building, nothing of that. Yet still the name St Ursula strikes a chord with me when I put it with the name of Wales. It will come to me. I will tell you before you leave us, I promise."

The meal in the refectory was plain but wholesome: the abbey's own vegetables, fruit and bread. Joslin noticed a monk who stood out among the white-habited Cistercians. He was a big man, strong, with a weatherbeaten face, as if he had spent much of his life away from the monastery. But what marked him out most was his habit. It was dark brown and looked strange amidst the white of the Cistercians, yet he spoke to everyone as if he knew them. Joslin wondered why a Benedictine was here among monks who lived by a different rule.

When the bells rang for the hour of Compline the Benedictine monk hurried away to prayers with the other monks. Afterwards in the guesthouse Joslin fell into conversation with him.

"Yes, I'm a Benedictine," said the monk. "I'm from Shrewsbury. My abbot has sent me on a journey, entrusting me with a message for a bishop. My name is Occa."

"And mine is Joslin. Joslin de Lay. I'm a minstrel."

Occa said nothing, but looked at him hard. Then: "Ah," he said. "I remember now. Your face worried me while we were eating. Seeing you close makes me sure."

"Sure of what?" said Joslin.

"That you nre French, a minstrel and surnamed de Lay," Brother Occa said wonderingly. "How extraordinary."

Joslin trembled. Time seemed suspended as if he was on the edge of another miracle. But Occa took his time.

"How extraordinary," he said again. "It must be nearly twenty years ago. I was a soldier once and I still mark time by the great battles. It was four years after Crécy and five before Poitiers. Having been a soldier means I can look after myself, so Abbot Geoffrey uses me as his messenger. Often, when I travel south, I stay here on my first night out and the last night before I reach Shrewsbury again. But that day, just as I was coming into Shrewsbury after a journey all through Wales from St David's, I was set on by robbers They took everything, put a knife through me and left me for dead. Then a French minstrel just like you came by. He saved my life. He carried me to the abbey and my brothers in the infirmary brought me to health again. The minstrel left next day, but not before I had opened my eyes, seen him and thanked him for what he'd done for me. I owed that man everything, for without him I would have been dead. I remember how he had carried a message all the way from France, just as I carry one now from Shrewsbury. But mine is for one bishop, while his was for all Welshmen. It came from someone whose name he did not say, though many of us guessed it. But the message was none of our business. The brothers showed him hospitality. Then they sent him on his way."

Joslin listened and could hardly speak. "Was his name Guillaume?" he finally managed to say.

"Yes," said Occa. "A monk doesn't meet many new people so the few he does meet stay long in his memory. Guillaume de Lay. How could I forget him? And you have a look of him about you which I can recognize, even after this great chasm of time."

Joslin gulped. "Where did he go after he left you?"

"I remember he said he was bound for Sycharth, once home to the princes of Powys, where their descendant Gruffydd Fychan now lives."

"Did he go there?"

"I don't know. We never heard of him again. He walked out of our abbey and, as far as we were concerned, out of the world."

"He was my father," said Joslin quietly.

"I think I would have known that, Joslin," said Occa.

Joslin could not sleep, comfortable though the bed was. He had wanted another miracle when he woke up in Llanfair Caereinion and now, before he slept in Strata Marcella, he had found it. The first trace of

Guillaume in Wales and the first inkling that his quest wasn't in vain. Dawn came and the bells of Lauds struck to mark the start of the monks' day. *"Sy-charth, Sy-charth,"* the bells seemed to say and the bells for Prime said the same.

Sycharth. They had to go there.

The innkeeper at Llanfair Caereinion looked at the two men facing him. One, with a sallow, marked face and a mouth twisted by disease, or as if a sword had slashed it, was not so bad, though the innkeeper wouldn't want to meet him on a dark night. But the other, with arrogant stare, lean face and sharp beard, stood for everything he hated. It wasn't just that he was English – this man was Norman through and through and almost smelt of William the Conqueror, even though three hundred years had passed.

"So where did they go?" the bearded one demanded.

"I don't know. I didn't ask."

"What did they do here?" said the one with the twisted lip.

"They asked for a priest."

"What for?" snapped the bearded Norman.

The innkeeper thought fast. "What would any young couple, riding in here hell for leather and come from who knows where, want a priest for? Obvious, isn't it?"

"Be careful how you speak, fellow," said the bearded Norman.

"Come on," said the twisted-mouthed man to his companion. "He knows nothing. We'll ask the priest."

But they got no further with the priest. He took one look and instinct told him that he must not give the true answer to their question. In these circumstances, he was certain that God would not mind a lie. He had the same idea as the innkeeper and gave them the same reply.

"They wanted me to marry them at once. I would not. So they went on their way."

The men looked at each other. "It's possible," said the one with the twisted mouth.

"If you weren't a priest, and I know how close your sort can be, I'd wrench more answers than that out of you," said the arrogant one and flicked the priest's face with his gauntlet as he strode out of the church.

Back at the inn, they demanded, "Which way did the couple go this morning? You must have seen that."

The innkeeper looked at them fearlessly, first twisted-mouth, then the bearded Norman, and knew that he would tell them another lie. "They went straight on," he said. "They carried on the road that brought them here, going north."

"You see?" said twisted-mouth. "I was right. The boy does know where he's bound for."

Before Joslin and Gyll left, Brother Jerome came to them. "I've remembered," he said. "I've seen it written somewhere, though I don't remember where and I cannot find it in my library. There's no church, no abbey or nunnery in Wales to St Ursula. But she has a shrine, a very tiny shrine, set up to her."

Joslin felt breathless. "Where is this shrine?" he managed to say.

"It's in Ynys Mon, Anglesey as the English say. An island at the very north-west tip of Wales, the seat of the princes of Gwynedd."

Ynys Mon. A strange conviction swept over Joslin. *The shrine in Ynys Mon is where I will find my answers.*

12

As they left Strata Marcella, Joslin had much to think about. Ynis Mon. Anglesey. His mother might be there. Nineteen years ago. Guillaume might have gone to Sycharth. Did he go to Anglesey and the shrine Brother Jerome spoke of? Then he thought of what the man with the twisted mouth had said. "*You'll find proof that I'm right.*" Did he mean at the shrine? No. Forget it. He was lying again.

Occa told them the way to Sycharth. By early afternoon they were in the valley of Afon Efyrnwy and crossing the river by a ford. They followed a track across the hills to Afon Cain and kept to this river's south bank until Llanfyllin. Here they stopped It was late afternoon on a bright, breezy day, though high clouds were sweeping in from the sea. A chill in the air hinted at bad weather to come. Occa had said that once in Llanfyllin they were near Sycharth, a few miles into the hills. Joslin wanted to press on.

"If Guillaume came to Sycharth, it was nineteen years ago," said Gyll. "His trail won't go cold tonight. There's no point in getting there in the dark, even if we find it. It's best to get a night's rest here and ask the way in the morning." Joslin knew she was right.

Llanfyllin was a busy little town clustered round St Myllin's church. They found an inn with room to spare and a landlord keen for an evening's entertainment when he saw Joslin's harp. So Joslin sang, French songs because nobody wanted English ballads here. As the people of Llanfyllin listened to his Breton lays and songs of Roland and Huon, keen eyes were watching. One man said to another, "The Frenchman sings well, but doesn't he put you in mind of that night years ago?" and the answer came, "Yes, he does. We'd fail in our duty if we didn't get back quick and tell our masters about him."

"It might be something, and it might be nothing," said the first.

"If it's nothing, well and good. If it's something and we've seen it and not told, it might go badly for us," said the other.

So they left the inn and followed dark ways which they knew as if it were day, to take this news to where Gruffydd and his son Owain lived, and where memories of the true Welsh princes still burned bright.

They were not the only ones riding through the night to Sycharth. The two men who had been in Llanfair Caereinion had argued. The arrogant man said, "I don't trust your instincts. The boy knows nothing."

"Nonsense," said the man with the twisted mouth. "Guillaume told him more than he's saying. Or something beyond himself pulls him."

"That low-born Frenchman blighted my life quite enough," said the bearded man. "Sooner or later, the boy must go to Sycharth, and I must be there, if only to see him and what he looks like."

"Why?" smiled the twisted-mouth. "Out of jealousy? Remember, *I* am the boy's father."

"So you say. If I thought it were true, I'd kill you now and leave your body by the roadside."

"Ah, but you don't know if what I say is true or not. Is he or isn't he my son? Which of us is he more like, Guillaume or me? How can you tell from such fleeting glimpses of him as you've had? But sons don't always take after their fathers. Who is his mother? He might take after her. That tortures you, doesn't it? But I'm important to you, so you daren't kill me. Besides, what does it matter who the boy's father is? You've been made to look a fool. You'd love to see my body rotting by the roadside. But you'll never see it. *You need me.*"

The arrogant man knew how right that was. He did need him – for now. When this business was over the old score would be settled.

He wheeled his horse round. "Just keep going the way your precious instinct tells you to," he snarled. "As for me, I'm going back to Sycharth, because I *know* he'll go there in the end."

"If you'd thought of that earlier, you'd have gone there straight from Dolforwyn Castle. All right, I'll tell you the whole awful truth."

So he did. The other listened to a tale of lies and deceit, then said, "Damn you. The boy should know," spurred his horse on and was gone.

The man with the twisted mouth watched him go, shrugged his shoulders and continued on his way.

But he soon stopped. Perhaps if things were going to happen at Sycharth he should be there to see. He had a great advantage over both his late companion and Joslin. He knew every inch of this country and could travel faster through it than either. It wasn't beyond his wits to follow them both. He laughed, turned his horse and cantered after his fast-disappearing ex-companion.

Joslin woke to thick cloud and driving rain from the west. "How do I get to Sycharth?" he asked the innkeeper.

"Why should you want to go there?" the innkeeper asked.

"I'm a minstrel," Joslin replied. "To play to the princes of Powys would be a great thing for me."

"Wouldn't you be happier staying with the likes of us?" said the innkeeper. "You don't need to worry if we don't like you. If Gruffydd and his son aren't pleased you might end up a sorry man."

"I'll take the risk," Joslin answered.

The innkeeper looked at him keenly. "I hope playing the harp's the only reason you're going there," he said.

"Why shouldn't it be?" Joslin asked.

The innkeeper shrugged his shoulders. "On your own head be it if it's not. Years ago, a French minstrel came to Sycharth and left turmoil behind him which some people may not have forgotten."

Joslin gasped. Gyll asked, "What do you mean, turmoil?"

The innkeeper looked at her and said, "The English are not always popular at Sycharth either."

"Gyll needn't fear while I'm here to watch out for her," said Joslin. He repeated Gyll's question. "What was this turmoil?"

"If you're only going to Sycharth to sing, it doesn't matter what it is. If you've another purpose then I'm not the man to tell you. I only speak from hearsay. Harm can come to rumour-mongers."

"How do we get there?" Joslin asked patiently.

"In this weather it's hard. Take the track over the mountains under Mynydd Mawr, though you'll never see its peak in this rain, until you come to Afon Tanat and Llangedwyn. Cross the river by the ford and strike eastwards into the hills. You'll find a fine palace with orchards and fishponds, a fit home for princes." He paused. "If they let you in, you'll have better lodging than I can give you."

"Keeping eastwards," said Joslin as they set off. "After three days of searching Wales I'm nearly back in England. I hope Occa was right."

They did indeed have a foul journey of it. Cold rain never stopped, the track was hard to follow, grey clouds were so low they could almost reach up and touch them. In mid-afternoon they forded Afon Tatan and found the tiny town of Llangedwyn. Here, a track headed upwards into woodlands. The woods were dark and dripping, but when they came out of the trees the sky was clearing and the sun struggling through the clouds to light up their first sight of Sycharth.

"Did Guillaume see what we're seeing now?" said Joslin.

Beyond the moat, earth wall, gatehouse and drawbridge was a high white cross set on top of a chapel. It towered over huddled houses and a hall. Beyond was a grassy mound, and on it a squat, bulky building of wood – a greater hall, fit for princes. Around the moat were broad, fenced fields where young corn grew and where hay was cut, orchards, a mill and a fishpond. The gatehouse was built of wood. The drawbridge was raised. They stood on the side of the moat and Joslin called, "I'm a travelling minstrel from France and I'm here with my lady."

A face looked out from a window space in the gatehouse over the drawbridge. "Your name?" its owner shouted.

"Joslin de Lay. My lady's name is Gyll and she's from England. Though we are not of Wales we bear no ill-will to the Welsh."

"You wish to play for the master of the house?"

"Yes."

"So do they all. Wait there."

There was a squeal of straining rope and the drawbridge came down. On the far side stood a grey-haired, bearded man with a cast in one eye. He wore the fur-trimmed robes of high office.

"You say you are a minstrel named de Lay?" he said.

"I do. I am," Joslin answered.

"My name is Rhys," the grey-haired man said. "I am my master's steward. Is mine a name which means anything to you?"

"No," Joslin replied.

"So you say now. Time will show if you tell the truth. Follow me."

So Gyll and Joslin followed Rhys into Sycharth, and, with every step they took, Joslin felt more sure that Guillaume had once walked here as well.

13

"Fetch grooms for their horses," said Rhys to the watchmen. "Keep watch on their belongings. I want no petty thievery. Don't gawp, minstrel. Follow me."

They passed houses, the chapel and the lower hall, and climbed steps up the mound to the great hall. Rhys moved nimbly, like a younger man. At the door into the hall, he said, "Wait there," and went inside. Appearing as if from nowhere, men with short swords stood near, not threatening but watching.

Soon, Rhys came back. "Enter," he said. "You're more privileged than most travellers. Gruffydd will see you, and so will his son Owain. Be careful what you say. Your talk will be like walking on eggshells."

He led them to a heavy door and knocked. He listened, then opened the door, stepped forward and spoke in Welsh to a big, strong man whose hair, like Rhys's, was grey. He sat in a carved chair, almost a throne. at his feet. Next to him sat a young man, Joslin's age, dark, keen-eyed. Gruffydd and his son

Owain – descendants of the princes of Powys, Joslin guessed.

"Kneel," Rhys whispered. "You're in the presence of princes."

They did so. Gruffydd laughed and said in English, "Stand up, minstrel and lady. Sadly we aren't princes any more, so I won't insult someone from France, and I won't annoy someone from England."

In spite of this friendly greeting, Joslin felt uneasy. Was he supposed to speak? What did Rhys mean by "thin ice"?

"So you're a minstrel and your name is de Lay," said Gruffydd. "Not a name often heard round these parts. Just once, as I remember. Did you ever know another minstrel of that name, Guillaume de Lay?"

Joslin's heart leapt. *Now* they were getting somewhere. "He was my father, my lord," he said, trying not to sound too excited.

"Was he now?" said Gruffydd. "So tell me, who is your mother?"

Gruffydd's voice and dark unblinking eyes told Joslin that this was not just a polite question.

"I don't know," he answered.

"Did you never see her Do you not even know her name?"

"My father never told me."

"Where is your father now?"

"Dead. He tried to tell me before he died. He didn't have time."

"It sounds as though he didn't die in his bed," said Gruffydd.

"He was murdered."

"By whom?"

Joslin nearly said, "a sallow, pockmarked man with a twisted lip", but remembered Rhys's "thin ice". "I do not know, my lord," he said.

"So, fatherless, and, for all you know, an orphan, you have come to Wales to look for work and make a new life. Or is there more?"

Joslin saw no harm in what he said next. "I'm looking for my mother, my lord." Did he imagine that Rhys stiffened and Gruffydd's eyes looked at him even more closely?

"Why should you think she is in Wales?" said Gruffydd.

"My father told me. It was the last thing he said before he died."

"I see. So where are you looking?" Gruffydd asked.

Joslin nearly said, "We're making for St Ursula's shrine in Anglesey." But he had so clear a feeling of cracking eggshells that a shiver ran up his spine. "We don't know where to look," he said.

"Did you expect to find her here in Sycharth?" said Gruffydd.

"No, my lord."

"Then why have you come here?"

"A monk from Shrewsbury told us my father was coming here when he left Shrewsbury Abbey. He had a message."

"The monk was right. Guillaume arrived out of the blue and we welcomed him. He ate with us, and then played and sang so well that people still talk about it."

"Where did Guillaume go next?" Joslin asked.

"I wish we knew, Joslin, I wish we knew."

Joslin risked a further question. "Why should my father come here? Was the message for you?"

"Did he not say? I suppose if he said nothing about your mother, he would hardly tell you that. Well, he did bring a message, though not just for me. It was given to him in France to deliver to all Welshmen. Of all the great houses in Wales, he came here first, but sadly, I was not best pleased to receive it. However, I said he could go on from here with his message to see what other men thought and, when he was ready, he went. But you'll have to travel a lot further to find out whether he did, I know for a fact that he never visited any of my neighbours. If you find someone who received the message, you may learn where he went and you might find your mother. Who knows?"

"What was the message, my lord?"

Gruffydd said, very quietly, "It would not be for your ears." The young man next to him shook his head and said, "It concerns his father and he has a right to know. If you won't tell him, Father, I will."

"Silence, Owain," said Gruffydd.

"Why? You've told me what it was and what it could mean for us. If it helps Joslin find his mother then he should be told as well."

"I said be quiet, boy," Gruffydd roared.

"I say you should tell him," said Owain. Joslin saw that Owain had rare strength and would not be denied, even by his father.

"Very well," said Gruffydd heavily. "Joslin, all is not well between Wales and England. The English have taken away our princes, laws, saints, all those precious things that made us different. If they could, they would take away our beautiful language. English kings want to rule everything they see: they have Wales already, they covet Scotland, they are fighting to make France their own. You and I both have little cause to love the English." Joslin cast a quick glance at Gyll. There was not a flicker on her face. "The wickedest cut is to have King Edward's son, the Black Prince, as Prince of Wales. He was given our land as a mere present, he's never been to Wales, he can't speak Welsh and he spends his time in France feathering his own nest and his father's cause. Welshmen long for a true prince, as we had until the English came a-conquering. There's a Welshman living in France. Like my son here, he is named Owain. Owain Lawgoch believes he is this longed-for deliverer. He is the last of the princes of Gwynedd, from the north. He wants to lead Welshmen against the English so that he can be the true Prince of Wales. And yet, like the present Prince of Wales, he's never been to Wales, can't speak Welsh and spends all his time in France. I ask you, Joslin de Lay, is that right?"

Joslin ventured an opinion, and never mind the eggshells. "Of course not," he said.

"Yet your father brought a message from that same Owain Lawgoch, calling his countrymen to take arms against the English. So your father would have disagreed with you there, wouldn't he?"

"I've never heard about any of this," Joslin replied.

"Why should Gwynedd take precedence over Powys? Why should I play second fiddle to this Owain Lawgoch? Answer me that, Joslin de Lay."

"They shouldn't. You shouldn't. I mean, I don't know," Joslin stammered. These really were eggshells.

Gruffydd suddenly smiled. "You have no idea, have you?" he said. "Neither did your father. He'd blundered into great matters way beyond him. Don't worry, I never kill messengers whose messages I don't like. I let Guillaume leave, after a night of song we'll never forget. In the end it seems he returned to France with a child he must have fathered on the way. But what did he do in the meantime?"

Joslin waited for Gruffydd to answer his own question.

"Do you know, Rhys?" said Gruffydd.

"I do not, my lord," Rhys answered stolidly. But the cast in his eye twitched and Joslin suddenly thought, *You do know.*

"One day, Owain Lawgoch will have prepared his army of Welsh and Frenchmen to sail across and beat the English out of Wales. What shall I do, Joslin? Shall I fight with my countrymen even though I don't want this man as my prince? Or shall I fight against them, because the English have been good to this family, and as the old rule says, if you cannot beat them, you should join them?"

"The answer will come clear one day, Father," said Owain.

"Perhaps so, but I may be dead and gone by then. And telling you my problem doesn't help you to solve yours, Joslin."

To Joslin's surprise, Gyll spoke. "My lord, when did Guillaume leave?" she asked. "Did he go next morning or did he stay a few days? Will anyone here remember him?"

104

Gruffydd looked at her sharply. Then he said, "What does it matter? He went when he was ready. It was a long time ago." His voice was curt, as if he didn't want to be bothered with the question. Perhaps, thought Joslin, he didn't think questions that women asked were worth answering. Or did he know perfectly well, and was he hiding something? Rhys's face was impassive but the flicker in his eyes was unmistakable. In his mind, Joslin put his suspicion into words – *Gruffydd knows when, and so does Rhys, and they don't want to tell us.*

The atmosphere had changed. Gruffydd's easiness had gone. Gyll and Joslin sensed they would soon be pushed out of his presence. Even so, he said, "Minstrel, you will play for us tonight, I trust?"

"Gladly, my lord," Joslin answered.

"Good. We shall look forward to it, and remember times when we were younger, and perhaps happier. And if I do not speak to you again, I wish you joy and success in your search."

"Thank you, my lord."

Gruffydd stood to go. But before he left, he asked a question which threw Joslin's mind back into turmoil. "Have you ever considered that Guillaume may not be your father?"

That awful word spoken by the man with the twisted lip echoed in his mind like a drum: *"Proof. Proof. Proof."*

When Joslin looked down from the minstrels' gallery to the long tables below, with Gyll beside him, Gruffydd high up at the far end and the rest of the household in its due order, he felt uncannily as if he were in his father's shoes nineteen years before. He had no idea that his songs were the same and that many older ones had their memories jogged. But first, he listened to a Welsh bard whose name was Iolo Goch, who earned Gruffydd's vast approval with a poem about Sycharth and its great wonders.

Near the end of Joslin's singing, there was a disturbance. The doors underneath the gallery opened with a crash and everyone turned to look, then fell silent. Solid leather boots smacked on the wood floor. Joslin saw the back of a tall man walking up the hall arrogantly, like a lord. He faltered, his voice died, he put down his harp. After the first gasp there was silence, then Gruffydd rose and said, "Edmund, my boy, how good to see you after all these years. Don't think that I hold the suddenness of your visit, interrupting delightful entertainment, against you."

"I am not your boy, Gruffydd. I have as much grey hair as you." The newcomer had the harsh voice of an English knight used to his own way. "If all were right, I should be your nephew. It still rankles with the Earl of March, my uncle, that I am not. I, Edmund Fitzgrace, have been insulted by your family. So have a care, Gruffydd."

"A care for what, Edmund?" Gruffydd asked mildly.

"For not harbouring traitors and spies. There's a spy and a traitor here, I believe, and he has his woman with him. Spies and traitors should be given up to me, and I'll not leave until that's happened."

"I know the business of everyone who enters these gates and I harbour no traitors nor spies, either for King Edward or against him."

Some people at the tables looked up at Joslin and Gyll and whispered. In a moment the newcomer would notice. Gyll crouched below the rail out of sight and Joslin did the same. They heard Gruffydd say, "My friends, the music is over for tonight. Edmund, come to my solar. Owain, Rhys, come with us. We need to convince our friend from England that we offer him nothing but good fellowship, with no secrets between us."

The four left the hall, then there was a burst of excited talk and the clatter of servants clearing the leftovers. Iolo Goch said, "I don't know what that was about, but I reckon it's you the Englishman means. If I were you I'd make myself scarce. Follow me."

So they did, up the staircase to the sleeping place where Guillaume had been so long before. Out of sight for a while at least, they sat down and considered what they had seen. Though they did not understand why, they knew that it was somehow very important – as well, they feared, as very sinister.

14

They crouched on the straw and considered the new turn of events.

"Who is this Edmund Fitzgrace?" Joslin wondered.

"He sounds like the de Novilles, and all their kind," Gyll answered.

How true, thought Joslin. He remembered Roger de Noville and the laughable trial that had nearly had him hanged. Edmund Fitzgrace had the same haughty tones, boding no good for French minstrels.

"We know that Guillaume was here twenty years ago," said Gyll. "He gave his message to Gruffydd and Gruffydd didn't like it. But Guillaume still sang for him, and that night was something no one will ever forget." She smiled. "As good as yours, Joslin."

"I think Gruffydd knows when and where Guillaume went," said Joslin. "I think Rhys does too. But after Rhys's warning about thin ice, something stopped me telling them about St Ursula's shrine. I was glad of that when Gruffydd asked if I ever wondered whether Guillaume was really my father. If Gruffydd knows the man with the twisted mouth, then this might be a dangerous place." He bunched his knuckles into a fist and beat his forehead. "Those four must be talking about me."

"Edmund wanted you," said Gyll. "It's not the first time you've been called traitor and spy. Are they bargaining for you?"

"Edmund may say I'm a spy, but he can't call me a traitor," Joslin replied. "If I were a spy, I'd be working for the king of France, so I'm no traitor to *my* country. But I don't understand how he knows about you."

"Has someone told him?" said Gyll. "The squire, perhaps, who escorted Lady Isobel?"

"Or the stalker who says he's my father?" said Joslin. "But if he did, they know our movements – we can't go anywhere."

"Why did Edmund say he should be Gruffydd's nephew?" said Gyll.

"Perhaps Gruffydd had a niece and Edmund wanted to marry her," Joslin answered.

"If so, he didn't," said Gyll. "Why not?"

They waited for two hours, with Iolo Goch snoring at the far side of the loft. Joslin muttered that they should get out and away from Sycharth, but wondering how made his mind seize up. Twice they heard bells ring the hour. The longer the wait, the more paralysed they seemed. Until . . .

There were footsteps below. Someone was climbing the staircase.

They froze like frightened rabbits. A light showed over the top of the steps and lit up a face, its owner's feet still on a lower rung. They knew that face: grey beard and hair, and a cast in one eye.

"Come with me," said Rhys. Joslin instinctively drew back.

"Don't you trust me?" said Rhys. "I don't blame you. Well, listen. You can't trust some people in Sycharth, but I'm not one of them. This is the second time in twenty years that I've climbed to the minstrels' loft and stood on the ladder looking in to bring a man called de Lay outside and set him on his way. Now do you believe me?"

Joslin, undecided, looked at Gyll by the light of Rhys's faint lantern.

"I believe him," said Gyll. "There's no choice."

So they rose up and followed Rhys down the steps, out of the hall through the kitchens, where banked-up fires smouldered and scullions slept in their warmth, then along dark corridors until Rhys opened a door. Outside, the night was cold and clear with a faint moon. They stood at the top of the stairway and looked out over Sycharth below.

"Don't move until you see the watchman pass below," Rhys whispered. "You'll have enough time to get down to the dovecote unseen. Your horses are by the stables, saddled and loaded up. Wait until the watchman goes past again. Then lead the horses past the dovecote and straight ahead. There's a place where you can get over the earth wall and ford the moat. It's the way your father took when he left. He had a guide, but I'm sorry that I can't find one for you."

"Why are you doing this?" said Joslin.

Rhys ignored the question. "Once you're over the wall, go fifty paces to your right where you'll find the path. Wait there and I'll meet you as soon as I can. I'll tell you all you need to know, about Guillaume, about what happened when he came here and who was his guide that night. I shall go now before I'm missed: you must find your way on your own." He dodged back inside and closed the door quietly. They heard a key grate in the lock.

They could see the dovecote below them and even thought they heard horses breathing. The watchman passed, so they crept down the stairway and the mound, ran to the dovecote and, on the far side, found Herry and Gib as Rhys had promised. Now they waited for the watchman to come back.

"What's that?" said Gyll suddenly.

"I don't know," said Joslin, but he felt an uneasy tremor. A faint cry had sounded from somewhere above them.

The watchman passed. He neither saw them nor, it seemed, heard the cry. "Perhaps it was a fox," said Joslin. "It's time to go."

Quietly and with infinite care, they led the horses to the moat. In spite of Rhys's assurances, the climb over the earth wall was difficult and the horses were unwilling. However, the moat on the other side was shallow and soon they were across.

"Now," said Joslin, "fifty paces to our right and we'll pick up the path." They counted them and found it showing faint in the brief moonlight through the clouds. They stopped and waited.

Nobody came. "Where is he?" said Joslin edgily.

"Be patient," said Gyll. "He said he'd be here when he could." Then she whispered. "There's something on the path ahead of us."

A black shape lay across the track, barring their way. "It's a fallen tree trunk," said Joslin.

"There are no trees here," said Gyll.

Suddenly, Joslin felt a sickening lurch in his stomach, because he knew what he was looking at. "It's not a tree," he said, and unwillingly approached it. His heart beat fast as he knelt and touched the object. It was soft – human skin with an ominous stickiness. He lifted his hand and saw what the stickiness was. The clothes, though, were sodden with water. He wiped his hand on the ground and looked up at Gyll.

"Dead," he said. "Murdered." He looked further. "Stabbed from behind. The coward's way. The clothes are wet. The body's been dragged through the moat." He looked up, his face despairing. "That cry," he said. "This is what it was."

"Who is it?" Gyll asked.

Joslin could see no features in the dark, but two things he was sure of. The body had a beard, and it wore the fur-lined robes of a steward, wet and bedraggled but unmistakable.

"Rhys," he said.

Gruffydd slept alone in the great bed. His wife was dead these eighteen years, but he had never got used to it. Now, ghosts from long past had come to worry him. The minstrel from France brought memories of that other minstrel who had arrived strangely, departed mysteriously and left such trouble behind.

Well, this young one thought the first minstrel was his father. And why shouldn't he? They had lived so long as father and son, they looked alike – and, now he thought about them, their faces and voices merged so that he could not tell one from the other.

And yet, and yet . . . Gruffydd had heard so much. There had been rumours, which, if they were true, meant the young minstrel had lived under a lie all his life. There had been plots, treachery – he no longer knew what was false, what was true. All he did know was that when Guillaume had crept away that night so many years ago, he left behind jealousy, spite, intrigue, double-dealing and an English knight angry enough to do murder. The flames had died, but Gruffydd knew the embers smouldered, and a tiny spark could set them blazing again.

He had an ugly feeling that this young Frenchman and his girl might be that spark. There would be no more sleep for him that night. He would wake Owain and discuss it. He was getting too old for these matters: Owain was strong, young and a fit descendent of the princes of Powys. If anyone should raise an army against the English, it should be him, not this mercenary chancer Lawgoch over in France.

He rose and padded out of his chamber, longing for peace of mind.

"What shall we do?" cried Gyll. For the first time since he had found her again, Joslin heard panic in her voice.

"Quiet," he whispered. "The killer can't have gone far. He may be close, watching us. We could be next."

So they stayed silent, trembling, clinging to each other. They strained their ears but there was no sound made by a human. They had a desolate feeling of Wales stretching away before them, miles of bare hills and mountains, dark, vast, unknown.

"Why kill Rhys?" said Gyll.

"To stop him telling us more, perhaps," Joslin answered. "But I don't understand why his body is left for us to see."

"We've got an enemy inside Sycharth and we're on our own again," Gyll whispered. "What shall we do? We can't leave the poor man here."

"We have to," Joslin replied. "We've got to get away."

"That's not right. It would be a sin. God would never forgive us."

"Look," said Joslin. "Ever since I came to England I've been in trouble. I kept finding dead bodies, and if I'd minded my own business and left them alone I'd have been here in three weeks, not ten months."

"Then murderers would have got away with their crimes and we wouldn't have met," Gyll replied.

"This is different," said Joslin. "We must get a good start in case we're followed."

"Oh, we're sure to be followed," said Gyll grimly. "Gruffydd will think we killed Rhys. The dogs will be out after us. Why don't we go back inside to the loft as if we didn't know anything had happened?"

Joslin said nothing for a while. Then he answered, "We'd never get back in. And even if we could, I don't want to spend any more time near Gruffydd or Edmund. Besides, I'm used to being hunted."

"At least let's put Rhys by the side of the path," said Gyll.

They did so and said prayers for his soul. Then they left.

Gruffydd came back to his chamber and sat on his bed, disheartened. Owain had not been helpful. "Father," he had said. "For all the honour I owe you, I must ask you to have nothing to do with this. These are matters of the past: failed uprisings, failed marriages, failed intrigues. Leave them be. We have better things to think about."

That was all very well, Gruffydd thought, but the past never went away, not in this unhappy land of Wales anyhow. It had a nasty habit of coming back and hitting you very hard when you didn't expect it.

15

It was not easy to ride the horses on this rough track in the dark. At first they climbed. Then Gyll said, "If we go down to our left, surely we'll come to that river, Afon Tanat."

Joslin agreed, and they carried on down the side of the valley. Clouds covered the weak moon. They listened for alarms at Sycharth to indicate a hunt setting out, but there was only the breathing and occasional bleating of sheep. Long before dawn they heard the river's fast-flowing waters. When they had passed over flat meadows to reach it, Joslin said, "If we could find a place to cross we'd put dogs off the scent."

"Not for long," Gyll answered.

"Long enough," said Joslin.

They walked by the stream until Joslin said, "Here."

The valley sides had closed in. On the far side, the land rose steeply. Water bubbled and foamed over stones: the stream was shallow enough to cross. They led the horses over and remounted on the other side. The going here was not as easy. Dark forests rose up, the nearest trees so close that they brushed at their elbows. When the moon shone through breaks in the clouds, they saw bare summits of mountains. The track was hard and the horses stumbled. Soon Gyll and Joslin dismounted again to lead them.

Then, as dawn came, the river divided. Two equal streams flowed away from each other, and the one on the far side carried on in flat, easy land.

"Shall we cross?" said Joslin. "It might be easier for the horses."

"If we keep on this side it might be easier for us," Gyll replied.

They did as Gyll said. The dawn did not chase away the clouds and the new day struck as chill as the night. When they looked ahead, their hearts sank. Mountains, bare, high, empty of life, rose up and stretched as far as they could see.

"We have to cross them," Joslin groaned. Then he realized something that he'd been half aware of for some time, and cheered up. "We aren't being followed. If they'd set up a hue and cry from Sycharth we'd have at least heard them. It must mean they don't think we killed Rhys. Perhaps they've found whoever did."

"Perhaps they don't know Rhys is dead," said Gyll.

"They must do. He's Gruffydd's steward, he has duties. A master depends on his steward."

They trudged on. The clouds never shifted. They crossed a ford to a town where they bought bread and a sharp-tasting cheese. The shopman, who spoke English, told them the town's name –

Llanhaeadr-ym-Mochnant – which was beyond them to repeat.

"We want to get to Ynis Mon," said Joslin.

"Then you'll have a hard time," the man replied. "The path you're on will take you up the river to the mountains. Keep on up the valley until the path gives out. You'll see rocks and screes in front, a high drop, and down it pours Pystyll Rhaedr, a great waterfall. It's a brave sight, but it's hard to get your horses round. If you manage to, you must keep going to the stone circle called Rhos y Beddau. Soon you'll come to a path to take you down a valley to Afon Dyfrdwy, or, as the English would say, the River Dee. If you take the left-hand road there, you'll come to a great lake and, leading away from it, a road to Ynis Mon. And I promise you, though there are still many miles to go, the worst of your journey will be over."

They thanked him and carried on their way. But before they had gone fifty paces, he called them back. "Forgive me," he said. "What was I thinking about? I've told you wrong. I gave you the way a sure-footed shepherd would take. It's too hard for those who don't know our land. Go back across the river and head along the road leading away from it."

"But that will take us out of our way."

"Trust me, it's easier, and with your horses you'll reach the true road across the mountains quicker. You'll join it at a place called Llangynog. You can't miss it. It's at the foot of a valley and you'll see the mountain Craig Rhiwarth guarding it on your right."

So they struggled back over the ford and set off down the road.

"Who would kill Rhys" said Gyll as they rode. "Not Gruffydd, surely. Owain, his son? If so, it must be a terrible thing to them for Rhys to let us out of Sycharth."

"I don't believe Owain would, even though Gruffydd didn't like the message Guillaume brought and my coming reminded him of things he'd rather forget," said Joslin. "They all say they don't know what happened to Guillaume after he left Sycharth, but I believe Rhys did. Perhaps he was killed to stop him telling us. Could Edmund have done it? I wish we knew who Edmund was, besides being an English knight."

"He thinks he ought to have been Gruffydd's nephew."

"Yes," said Joslin thoughtfully. "That might mean we're right about Gruffydd having a niece . He tried to make a match between her and Edmund but she wouldn't marry him."

"Wouldn't it be strange if Grufyyd's niece was your mother?" Gyll replied and laughed. "Wouldn't you feel good to think that your mother preferred a wandering French minstrel to an English nobleman?"

"Yes," said Joslin. "I would. But I keep remembering what that man said. I'd find proof he was my father and I wouldn't be able to deny it."

"You mustn't believe him," said Gyll.

They rode on. Then Gyll said, "Joslin, have you remembered any more since your dream by Strata Marcella?"

"No," he replied. "But I know I will, all in good time."

Some time later, Gyll asked, "When Guillaume was killed, you said English lords had come to the castle. What did they come for?"

"I don't know," said Joslin. "English lords had never been before. They must have had some business with the count, to do with the war."

"But the man with the twisted mouth was there. Is he a lord?"

"I've no idea what he is."

"And was Guillaume really frightened when he saw them?"

"Yes. He hid in his room. But sometimes we were seen together, and I felt that everybody was looking at us. The man with the twisted lip was the worst. I had bad dreams about him."

"You never told me that," said Gyll. "But perhaps it wasn't just him your father was frightened of. Was Edmund there?"

Joslin conjured up lean, haughty countenances, no different from the faces of the French nobles they were eating and drinking with, yet hostile and forbidding. He recalled loud voices expecting obedience. Sometimes he was sure that bearded, cruel face had been in the castle, sometimes he felt it hadn't. It was too long ago, and besides, like Guillaume, he had been keeping out of their way.

"Perhaps he was," he said. "I'm not sure."

"I wonder if . . ." Gyll started, then tailed off.

"Go on," said Joslin.

"Something Gruffydd said. This Owain Lawgoch who originally gave Guillaume the message is getting an army together to drive the English out. Some are Welsh, some are French. Perhaps it was

120

about that – the English lords were trying to stop the French helping the Welshmen."

"If it was, it links Guillaume with them, and would give them reason to want him dead," he said. "But if that's why they killed him I've been wrong all this time. I thought it was to do with my mother."

"It might still be," said Gyll. "Owain's message brought Guillaume here, but it seems a lot more happened to him."

Joslin looked up. By the track to their right were clumps of trees and towering away from them were two mountains, brown and purple, their tops lost in low cloud. Rocky outcrops broke the colour and he remembered the man who had told them the way – "*Rocks and screes . . .a high drop and down it pours Pystyll Rhaedr, a great waterfall.*" What else did he say? "*A circle of stones.*" Between the mountains was a valley with a stream pouring down. He imagined leading horses across such country, the cold night coming on, lost, without bearings. The shopman knew they'd never make such a journey. If they could reach – what was it called? – Llangynog? – by evening they would have done well.

Gyll disturbed his thoughts. "Look behind you," she said.

He turned. About three hundred paces behind was a figure on horseback. He had a sudden sinking of the heart. Even at this distance he knew who the figure was: something about the way the horseman sat, some indefinable instinct that here was danger. "It's him again. My false father," he said. "He must have been behind us for hours." And he'd had no idea – his instinct for being stalked had let him down. The man should be miles away, following a non-existent trail. "He doesn't have to catch us up. He knows we'll stop sooner or later and this place Llangynog can't be far away."

Ahead of them the track turned right and for a while the way behind would be hidden by trees. They would not see the man, but neither would he see them. Joslin thought of a plan, shadowy and desperate. "We'll get off the horses and walk, and let him see us doing it," he said. They did so, and Gyll looked questioningly at him. "I'm going to leave you for a while," he went on. "I'll hide in the trees and wait until he's well past, then make off into the mountains. You carry on into Llangynog and ask for sanctuary in the church. The priest will help you. Stay there until I come for you. Perhaps he'll go straight past."

"But he's not stupid. He'll know what we've done. He'll catch me. He might *make* me tell me him where you are."

"Then tell him . . . oh, I don't know. You'll think of something."

"Joslin, you can't leave me like this. It's a foolish plan."

"Think of a better," he said.

"Give me time," she said.

"We haven't got any time," cried Joslin and then he was gone, into the trees and out of sight. She nearly called, "Joslin, come back", but bit the words back. Mad idea though it was, she wouldn't give him away.

She took Herry's reins and led both horses on, walking in front and hoping that the horses would hide Joslin's absence. After some moments, she risked a look back. The man was still there, also leading his horse, keeping his distance. Soon she came to Llangynog and its little church, set at the entrance to a valley. On their right, the mountain Craig Rhiwarth brooded. Gyll tied the horses up outside the church and went in. A priest was praying at the altar. She waited until he had finished, then said, "Father, I crave sanctuary."

"Of course, my child," said the priest.

Joslin, hiding in the trees, watched the man pass by. *He means to corner us in the town, he thought. He must know this land so well that if he thinks there's no way out for us, he's right.*

When man and horse were well past, Joslin set off, climbing through the trees until he emerged on the side of a valley with a stream bucketing down it. To his left, Craig Rhiwarth stood over him, its grey rocky outcrops like watchtowers from which sentries might see his every move. Opposite was another mountain. All else was purple, green, brown – heather, gorse, bracken and short well-cropped grass, flecked with grey rocks poking through the soil's thin surface. He struggled up to the head of the valley and, gasping for breath, looked down. So desperate was he to get away that he hadn't realized what a steep climb he'd made. Now, in solitude and silence except for curlews crying and an occasional far-away bleat, he wondered why.

Sudden disgust with himself rose up and nearly choked him. This was no brilliant idea. He'd run away and left Gyll alone to deal with a dangerous enemy. "*You can't leave me like this. It's a foolish plan,*" she had said. And he hadn't listened.

"I'm being followed and I need God's protection," Gyll said.

"I understand," the priest answered. "The world is full of wicked men. I will take you to my cottage where I promise that you'll be safe"

He untied Joslin's horse and Gyll untied Gib. As they led them from the church, he asked mildly, "Why do you have two horses, my child?"

"My friend fears the man who follows us. He left me," Gyll said.

The priest sniffed. "Perhaps you're better without such friends."

Gyll did not answer. As she entered the cottage, she heard the clop of horse's hooves. She turned. The pockmarked man was looking straight at her. He laughed, a sharp, contemptuous laugh. Then he mounted his horse, pulled it round and disappeared the way he came.

They were finished. He knew what Joslin had done and she couldn't help him now.

He had to go back, find Gyll, say, "You were right. I didn't think properly. Forgive me. We'll face him together."

But he must hurry. Dusk was coming. Up here the clouds seemed lower: a night on this wide treeless moorland would be exposed and very cold. A chill wind pierced his thin tunic and dug into his bones. He looked back and his heart sank. Far below, emerging from the trees, was that familiar figure. He *knew*. Being followed by him was having a devil on your back. With nowhere to hide, all he could do was run across the bare moor, further and further away from Gyll and all hope.

Then the questions came. How did the man know where to look? Had Gyll betrayed him? No, she'd never speak against him. His heart like lead, Joslin realized that this man seemed able to read his mind. There was no escape, in dreams or in life.

Had the man seen him? Perhaps not: dark was coming fast. If he went back he would be cut off so easily that he might as well give himself up now. He must keep going. He stumbled on across the rocky ground, falling, picking himself up, wet-footed, cold, shivering, further away from Gyll with every step. All he could hear was his heart thumping in his chest and his own retching breath. Soon it was dark, and a cold drizzle started. The moon was hidden and there were no lights from village or even shepherd's hut. If hell is wet, he thought, then I'm in it.

He stumbled again, went sprawling, and this time stayed down until his breathing subsided. When he picked himself up, he saw that he had fallen over a huge stone set in the ground, much larger than the little rocky outcrops he'd dodged all this time. It could almost have been put there deliberately and it stirred an old memory. Glad of something else to think about, he tried to recall it.

Ah, yes. Back in France, he had often been with Guillaume when the count took his retinue to visit other noblemen, and sometimes they travelled westwards into Brittany. There, he had seen many stones like this – he remembered especially Carnac, with its strange rows of stones, stone upon stone, standing like soldiers. Who put them there? Why?

Nobody knew, but the folk told tales about them, how giants set them up and fairies danced round them, how they were sacred places long before the Church came to France, and to many they still were, even though the Church tried to stop them.

Then he recalled the man who told them the way that morning. "*A great waterfall . . .* "he'd said, and then "*a stone circle...*" He had given names to both, but Joslin could not remember them. This must be the stone circle. For a moment, now he had something else to think about, he forget his pursuer

He peered into the darkness. There was another stone a few paces to his right, yet another to the left. Together they gave him his bearings. He walked to the right-hand stone. From it, he could see another, then another. Soon he had paced out the whole circle. Then he paced across it. Thirty good paces in diameter. As well as that, there were two lines of stones, like a little avenue, leading to it.

So, as with Carnac and the stones all through Brittany – had giants brought them? Well, the Welsh said this was the place of the giant Berwyn, whose chair was on top of the highest mountain nearby. Were the stones sacred? What was this place called? He tried to hear again the voice of the man of the morning. *What was this place called?*

Had he spoken aloud? At any rate, a voice, coming from behind him and whispering almost in his ear, said, "It is called Rhos y Beddau."

The priest showed Gyll to a little room with a low pallet made up with mattress and sheets, for travelling guests. "I shall not ask what trouble you are in, my child," he said as he left her. "But I will pray for you, nevertheless."

Whatever prayers he, or Gyll herself, had said, they didn't help her to sleep. This was the first night she had been truly alone since she left Stovenham with the Lady Isobel and only now did she consider what had happened to her. Providentially, she was with her Frenchman, something she had dreamed of hopelessly for months. She had listened to everything he'd told her and realized how much he didn't understand himself. But what did she really *know* about him? Before this amazing encounter in Wales, she had seen him – how many times? Once as a prisoner in the castle at Stovenham, once when he was brought out to be hanged, once when she had rescued him and they had kissed before he plunged off into the night, then that extraordinary time when the murderer was uncovered and the de Noville family was destroyed, and, last of all, before Joslin left for London with Alys, and Gyll was resigned to him leaving only dreams behind. Had she found her long-lost true love, or was he just a plank to cling to like a drowning sailor.

And now he had left her, followed by the man he feared so much. Would someone who really loved her have done such a thing? He might never come back. Perhaps this man would kill him. Perhaps he would die alone on those high, cold slopes. She would never know, and would live alone again, trapped among alien people, with no one to talk to but a priest who at least spoke English.

Her thoughts slipped into despair. It stifled her like a pillow pressed on her face. She fell into a deep, dark and merciful sleep.

She woke again, suddenly. She sat up, wondering what had roused her.

It took her a moment to know and when she did she almost laughed. Her despair had gone. She was thinking clearly. An idea had come, so intriguing that it had broken her sleep. Carefully, she went through it, to see how good it was. When Joslin slipped away into the woods, he had left his horse behind. After the pockmarked man had seen her, laughed and turned round, he still rode his horse. His laughter must have meant that he knew what Joslin would do and where he would leave the road. Yet if Joslin wouldn't ride a horse up the slopes, then neither would the pockmarked man. He must have left his horse somewhere – hidden among the trees, perhaps, waiting for his master to come back.

But if she went out early in the morning, found the horse and led it away where the pockmarked man couldn't find it, then when Joslin came back they could ride away fast and leave the man miles behind.

Was that a good idea? The horse might not be there. Joslin might not come back. But the man might, and when he found her he might take a terrible revenge.

Did that matter? She realized that if Joslin didn't come back, the man could do what he liked, because she wouldn't care any more.

16

"Yes. Rhos y Beddau," it repeated. "I've no doubt you'll have seen such places where you come from."

Joslin would not answer.

"Have you?" It sounded more threat than question.

Joslin nodded.

"That's better," the voice said. "I don't care how you choose to communicate with me, as long as you do, somehow. Sadly, there are some sons who don't speak to their fathers. I'm sorry if you're one of them, but time will change that. One day we'll be friends, you mark my words."

Joslin nearly said, "You're not my father" again. But perhaps this man was goading him into talk. If he kept quiet, he'd have an advantage – small, but nevertheless something to cling to.

"Yes, such places as these. What are they, Joslin? Who arrived here so many years ago and set them in the earth? The giant Berwyn, perhaps? Who knows?"

Joslin stayed resolutely silent.

"What are they for? These stones, are they altars? They're to no god that we know, I'll be bound. How many old Druids stood in this ancient place performing the rites their religions demanded, I wonder?"

Not a flicker from Joslin. The man waited for Joslin to break, but he stayed firm. The only sound was the night breeze rustling gorse and heather. Then came another sound, insistent, filling Joslin's ears. It took a moment to know what it was. Breathing – short and quick as if the man was getting angry. Joslin wondered: should he be afraid?

No, he should feel a small triumph. If the man was angry, he was unsettled: Joslin had gained some sort of upper hand.

He felt strong fingers on his shoulder. The voice, calm no longer but hissing with fury, said, "Face me!" The fingers twisted him round. He was forced to look straight at that all too familiar face. The eyes glittered, almost lighting up the features.

The man's breathing eased. "There, that's better. Now you can see me close to. You're flinching from these terrible marks on my face and this ghastly twisted mouth. But if I didn't have them you'd see how alike you and I are. You wouldn't doubt who your father is then."

Joslin clamped his lips tight together.

"Still silent? Ah, you're overcome with filial love and remorse at how you've treated me. I understand, and I forgive. As for the pockmarks, plague and pox over many years leave their mark. I don't complain: many have worse than this. But the twisted mouth – there I do complain. I don't suppose you know how I got it."

No answer.

"Well, I'll tell you something that villain you thought was your father never would. *He* did it to me, Joslin. A cowardly attack when I was defending an innocent girl against his wild rage. He came at me like a mad beast. I was unarmed but I fought him off: he lunged at me with a wicked blade, a vicious slash meant to have my throat out. Instead, he sliced my lip open so it never healed properly."

Joslin looked at him unblinkingly, like stone.

"Yes, a wicked blade, glinting as if flashed down on me. In fact, *this* blade." With a lightning fast movement he seized Guillaume's dagger from Joslin's waist. Joslin staggered back and fell against a standing stone. Spreadeagled over it, he looked up at his tormentor.

"Yes, this blade. It was never his. Did he tell you who owns it?"

Joslin still made no move or sound.

"I see that he didn't. Neither will I.

Except that a better man than he lent it to him, as a token of a job that Guillaume vowed to complete. But though Guillaume pledged his honour, *that job was never done.* The dagger was a sign of his promise. But he broke the promise, negligently and treacherously. What do you think of a man like that?"

The goading worked at last. "You're lying," Joslin gasped.

"Lying, am I? Then you must prove it. With Guillaume dead, you can't. But I can. I'm telling the truth, and sooner or later you'll have to accept it. One day soon you'll see what my proof is, and then you'll understand once and for all that your life so far has been based on a lie."

Joslin's silence was well broken now. "You've got *no* proof," he screamed. "Guillaume's dead because you killed him. I don't know what you were to him and I don't even know your name, but you killed him."

"Oh, Joslin," said the man pityingly. "Why should I want to kill Guillaume? We were friends at first. And it's no use for me to tell you my name. It would mean nothing. Most people wouldn't know who you meant, because they would know me by another. I have many names. In my business you keep ahead of your enemies."

"Then what name did Guillaume know you by?"

"A fair question. He knew me as Lamb. James Lamb."

Joslin quickly searched his memory. No, Guillaume had never mentioned that name.

"And the woman you're searching for really is your mother," said James Lamb. "Guillaume lied about who your father is. She loved me, Joslin, not him. But there was a third man, and she fled from him too. Three men wanted her and she rejected two. Think of that, Joslin."

Joslin thought of a woman rejecting two men, and it rang a bell in his mind. The blessed St Ursula of the shrine he was bound for wouldn't marry a pagan prince or the chief of the Huns. She also rejected two other men. He remembered sitting on the Black Mountain on his first day in Wales, wondering if his mother had done the same as St Ursula but, unlike her, had loved a third.

"Who was this third man?" Joslin asked.

"I'll never tell you that," said James Lamb. "All I say is – if you ever meet him, keep out of his way. Next to him, I really am a lamb."

Then Joslin's heart leapt. He had an advantage. He knew who the third man was. "Is his name Edmund?" he said.

It was as if he had hit James Lamb between the eyes. He blinked, then muttered something under his breath. Joslin needed a musician's sharp hearing to know what he said – "Rhys. I should have known."

So – Edmund was the third man in his mother's life, and James Lamb thought Rhys had told them. Did he know Rhys was dead?

James Lamb had recovered his composure. He looked at Joslin with a half-smile on his lips. He was balancing Guillaume's dagger between his hands, lovingly stroking the blade. "I wonder," he said.

"You wonder what?" said Joslin.

"Whether after all this time we've come to the end of the road. To me, you seem very stubborn. I've told you the truth about Guillaume and you won't believe me. I've said there's proof, but you won't listen. I've offered you a father's love and security, but you'll have none of it. I hoped we would find your mother, you and I, and face her together, me a long-lost husband and lover, you a born-again son with his own true love. But it won't do, will it? My dream is born to die, because you'll have none of it. If you won't believe it, then it's no good. What's the point of going on? No, best to make an end of it now."

"What do you mean?" said Joslin.

"You know the story of Abraham and Isaac?" said James Lamb.

"Of course. Abraham took his son Isaac up into a high place and then he . . . " Now he knew what the man meant, and his voice died.

"Yes, Joslin. A high place, like this. A place of sacrifice. What do you think the Druids did on these stones? They made sacrifices to their gods. Young men, young women, it didn't matter. If the gods wanted them, they had them. And it's the same for our own jealous, angry God. He demands blood sacrifices – however dear to us, if God wants them, they are His. So Abraham came to a high place to sacrifice his own son."

"But he didn't," said Joslin. He felt very calm. "An angel told him that God spared his son after all, and gave him a sheep to sacrifice instead."

"But I don't want to sacrifice a sheep, Joslin. And how likely is it that an angel will suddenly come to stay my hand now?"

Joslin couldn't help looking round. The moorland remained empty.

"Even if one did, I'd take no notice. 'm not Abraham." He pushed Joslin back, spreadeagling him over the stone again. The blade glinted and James Lamb's eyes glinted with it.

"I'm not Isaac," said Joslin, staying calm, looking straight into those glittering eyes. "This isn't a sacrifice. This is murder. I've seen terrible murders in the last months, but this would be the very worst of all."

"Would it Oh, thank you, Joslin. Having seen what you've seen and been through since Guillaume died, I'm quite honoured to hear that."

James Lamb pushed Joslin down further so that his head fell back, exposing his throat. Joslin saw the blade above him. He closed his eyes and heard James Lamb say, "This is the end of your road, Joslin de Lay."

Dawn broke. The previous day's cloud and drizzle had gone. There was a fresh breeze and morning chill. Life in the village was stirring and Gyll was woken by sunlight. She recalled her great idea at once. She went through it again, then got out of bed to carry it out.

The old priest was up already and had been saying mass in his church while Gyll still slept. "Good morning, my child," he said.

"Father, I'm going out to look for my friend. I worry for him."

"I hope he is worth it," the priest replied.

Gyll walked out of Llangynog, following their way in, until she came to the trees where Joslin had run off. Somewhere here, she thought. And that man would leave the road near here as well. She listened. She heard rustling, then breathing and a champing noise, like a horse eating. She crept into the trees.

Yes, there he was: a black horse, tied to a tree, eating leaves. He must be standing where he had been left the night before, waiting patiently for his master to return. He saw her, whinnied and skittered backwards. Gyll reached out and he backed away further. She ran out into the open, picked up handfuls of grass, ran back and offered them. He lifted them off her hands with his rough, warm, tongue.

"There, isn't this better than leaves?" she said, and stroked his muzzle. He whinnied again.

She wondered if she dare untie him. He was tall, strong, a horse for knights, not jailers' daughters. But she must, or why bother coming?

Then she heard more noise. Someone was approaching fast through the trees. "The man," Gyll gasped. "He's back."

She slipped behind a tree trunk. The noise came nearer. She heard footfalls, sobbing, gasping breath: she made out a figure almost bent double, swaying, blundering, careering through the trees. She waited for him to come close, take his horse, mount it and gallop away.

The figure burst out of the trees in front of her. It wasn't the man. It was Joslin.

She couldn't believe it. But why shouldn't it be Joslin? He was just as likely to come back, wasn't he? He looked in such a state that the man must be chasing him. "Joslin?" she called.

He stopped, looked round dazedly, then saw her. "Gyll!" he cried, plunged towards her and fell into her arms. "Gyll, oh Gyll," he gulped. "I – I think I've killed him."

17

Joslin was pale and trembling. Retching breaths from deep in his chest. racked his whole body. Gyll had seen him face fear, but never like this.

"Don't speak," she whispered, and put her arms round him to bring back warmth. She held him close until his breathing eased. Then she untied the black horse. Holding its reins with her left hand, she put her right arm round Joslin's waist and they walked slowly back to the village and the priest's house. The priest had gone out. Gyll led Joslin into her room, sat him on her bed and said, "Tell me what happened."

"I think I killed him," Joslin gasped. His face was deathly pale.

"Don't tell me the end. Start from the beginning."

So Joslin told her about climbing to the high moor, seeing his pursuer far away, finding the standing stones, that sudden, ominous voice and their alarming conversation.

"He said that Guillaume knew him as James Lamb," he said. "I don't know if that's his real name.

Oh, but he wanted me dead. He would have cut my throat on those stones. The blade was ready and my throat was bared. That blade – Guillaume's blade, *my* blade."

"Then why didn't he?" Gyll asked quietly.

"Suddenly I didn't care if he did. I'd done all I could and it wasn't enough. I was trapped up there and you were lost to me. Why shouldn't I die? Then I thought of what he'd do when he'd killed me. He'd search my body. He'd find the locket, Guillaume's locket. He'd take it to my mother. I don't know what's in it, but it was important to Guillaume, and to her, and it matters to me as well. I thought of James Lamb, finding her, showing her the locket and the dagger. How would she feel after so many years, to see these tokens brought to her by this imposter who says he's my father? couldn't let it happen, Gyll. I was filled with four men's strength. I don't know where I found it. Well, yes I do. God and the thought of you and Guillaume's spirit gave it to me. I launched myself at him, head, legs, body, knees. I sent him sprawling. Then I ran, hoping I was heading back the right way. But in the dark, one way's like another. He'd got up and was after me. I just ran.

"I heard roaring. I thought it was in my head. But it was real and got louder. Just in time, some providence made me stop short. I was on the edge of a great drop, with rocks and crags below me and a huge waterfall to my left. Do you remember the shopman? He told us about a stone circle and a great waterfall. Well, I'd nearly died on the stone circle and now I nearly died falling over the waterfall. And it *was* a great waterfall, Gyll. It cascaded from ledge to ledge, rock to rock, and anyone caught in it would be dashed to death in the foam so far below.

"He was running at me with the dagger in his hand. He meant murder, Gyll. I saw his eyes glaring and foam flecking his mouth. He flung himself at me, not caring if he stabbed me or hurled me over the edge. But I fought. I wanted my father's dagger back and him out of my life. We struggled on the edge. I know he was stronger, but I wasn't going to be killed by him, not now. Often I thought I was gone and I heard him laugh, but each time I somehow pushed him back and then I turned him so he was on the edge and I wondered, *could I?* And just as I wondered – *Gyll, he was gone.* I looked over the edge. I couldn't see him. He was over that drop, and Guillaume's dagger with him. I thought of him bouncing down from ledge to ledge, his body ruined on hard stones and drenched with foam, and all I could say was, 'Thank you God, for not letting it be me.' "

He stopped and put his head in his hands. Then he looked up and said, "Gyll, what am I going to do? All this while I've lived with murders and brought the true reckoning for the killers themselves, and now I've made myself as bad as they are".

She stroked his forehead and said, "How can you be? It was you or him." He didn't answer.

"You need more comfort than I can give you," she continued. "Wait for the priest, then tell him everything. He'll give you absolution – God's forgiveness."

Joslin looked up gratefully. "Yes," he said. "Perhaps he will."

When the priest came back, Joslin asked to see him alone. They went into the old man's private room and Gyll waited outside. When Joslin emerged, she did not ask what had happened but saw that he looked much happier.

"Now," he said. He sounded almost like his old self. "To Ynis Mon. And let's not waste a moment, now there's no one to follow us."

They were on their way within the hour. The old priest watched the young man with his harp and the dark-haired girl who cared for him so much and wondered if he would ever be called to account for the secret from the confessional which he now possessed and the presence of a proud black horse in his field.

Now the weight of guilt was off his shoulders and he didn't have to look behind him, Joslin felt light-hearted. The horses made good progress through the deep valley, Cwm Rhiwarth. After four miles the valley sides flattened and the landscape changed to rolling hills and woods, with a few settlements of stone cottages with turf roofs. In mid-afternoon they came to Afon Dyfrdwy, the River Dee. By early evening they reached the eastern tip of a great lake, called Llyn Tegid in Welsh, and soon they were in Bala. Joslin felt a slight qualm of fear: with its straight streets, shops and many of the voices he heard, he could tell this was a town built by the English. But Gyll squeezed his hand and whispered, "Don't worry. Nobody will notice us."

They came to the chapel by the town cross, and looked up and down the High Street. "There's an inn," said Gyll, pointing.

"I'll hide my harp," Joslin answered. "I won't sing here. We must stay unnoticed."

The inn was comfortable, the beds were soft. Joslin was tired after his night of near death. But Gyll said, "We're no more than two days away from Ynis Mon. We must think about what we'll do when we're there."

"I can't," said Joslin. "I have to sleep."

"Then try to dream again. You've done it once and remembered things you'd forgotten. Think again about what you started remembering before we came to Strata Marcella."

"I can't," Joslin replied. "I must sleep, I must..."

"Think," insisted Gyll. "Think back." And she turned those deep grey eyes on him which always made his heart leap and, as he closed his own eyes, he thought, *Yes, I will.*

The dream was clear as day, yet strange as a ballad of faeryland. Just as when he had been taken into lost memories before, he was very small again. But this time he was neither wet nor frightened. There was sunlight, warmth, security and love. He heard a woman's voice singing. Was she singing to him? He heard no one else, because this was the only voice he wanted to hear. The melody was such as would stay in the mind for ever: it was one he had often since played and sung himself and put words to, had wondered where it came from and marvelled at the ease with which it formed itself under his hands and in his voice. The words meant nothing to him. Yet, somehow, their shape, their sound, spoke to him of love, comfort, infinite protection. He wished he could stay asleep and listen to this song for ever. Even as he framed the wish, he knew his dream was going to end.

He opened his eyes and saw a face that was beautiful, framed in dark, dark hair, with eyes gentle and calm. In his sleep, he knew this was his mother. The voice, sweet, lulling, carried on. He saw beyond her face. He was in a great hall, a castle. He saw banners hanging from high walls. And then, as before, there was no sunlight. Instead, he was in darkness, smelt damp salt; and heard the creaking of wood strained to breaking. Nothing staying still, least of all his own stomach This was a world with no order, nothing to cling to. Except that soon, and as before, there *was* something to cling to: a strong arm and a well-loved voice – not a woman's, but a man's, which he did understand. "Be still, Joslin. You're safe." And then the voice said something else, which Joslin could not quite hear.

When he woke, he told Gyll.

"What do you think it means?" she said.

"I was in a ship again," he replied. "But before that I was with my mother. She sang. It was in Welsh. No wonder when I first heard a Welshman sing I though it was how angels would sound."

"Then perhaps you weren't taken to France as soon as you were born? Your mother knew you and you knew her."

"I remembered the ship which took me to France," said Joslin. "But I was in a castle before, with her. The count's castle at Treauville, surely. So how can I have sailed to France if I was already there? The man's voice was Guillaume's. I know that now. He said something else. I wish I knew what it was. If I could just get that little bit further . . ."

"You will," said Gyll. "The memories will return."

"Perhaps," said Joslin. But remembering what Guillaume might have said was like trying to look through a stone wall.

The friendly innkeeper, a Welshman who spoke English, told them the way. "Make from here to Ffestiniog," he said. "Keep going west towards the sea and sands of Tremadog Bay, but at Penrhyndeudraeth strike north again and follow the pass of Aberglaslyn, between the high mountains. You'll leave Yr Wyddfa, or as the English say, Snowdon, on your right. I believe you'll be at Afon Menai by tomorrow evening and you'll see Ynis Mon across the water." He narrowed his eyes and looked at the two of them carefully. "You'll also see King Edward's great castle at Caernarfon, and if that doesn't appeal to you I suggest you should find a boat to take you across Menai from somewhere else."

They thanked him, saddled up the horses and were away and out of Bala early. The road stayed firm: the sun shone fitfully through scudding clouds. They made good progress, ever climbing, back into wild, high country, and with every hoofbeat Joslin's heart quickened at the thought of the questions that might soon be answered.

18

In Penrhyndeudraeth that evening they were surrounded by Welsh folk. England seemed far away and Joslin felt safe. When they stopped in the centre of the tiny town, Joslin suddenly didn't care about being known, He took his harp from his back, started to play and sing and was surrounded by listeners. As he sang, he wondered if tonight would be the last time that he would sing on his long quest. Tomorrow they might find St Ursula's shrine, and with it his long-lost, long-dreamt-of mother.

So he sang every song that had buoyed him up since he came to these islands: Sir Orfeo, The Tournament of Tottenham, then his old friend Crispin's favourites, Gamelyn and The Carl of Carlisle, ballads from France, Lai le Freine and many others. Then, coming as sudden and fresh in his memory as if he was still listening to it, he sang the angelic Welsh song Dafydd had played, so long ago it seemed now, in Henley, on the way to Oxford. The people loved them all, whether the English, French or Welsh, and Joslin sang without thought of payment. By midnight, his fingers were sore and his voice was giving out. But then there was no shortage of offers of good food and drink and comfortable beds for the night.

When Joslin slept, he hoped he would dream his buried memories again, his mother and the mysterious voyage. But no. The sallow pockmarked face and twisted mouth of James Lamb appeared instead, mocking him as he had in dreams night after night on his journey and as they had once mocked Guillaume. In this dream, he shouted, "Go away. You're dead." But the face smiled more teasingly than ever and Joslin woke, hearing the echo of his own voice shouting, "Go away You're dead."

He is *dead. He* has *to be dead,* he thought. *I saw him fall and disappear over that terrible edge.* He lay for some time trying to calm himself, then slipped back into sleep. He didn't see James Lamb any more – but he didn't see his mother either.

Next day, remembering what the innkeeper at Bala had told them, they headed towards the sea until the land flattened out, they smelt salt in the wind and the road turned right by the side of Afon Gwyrfal. Soon they were indeed among the mountains. The skies were grey, the wind piercing and bitter, for all that it was July. Thick woods reached down to the road and sometimes the river widened into broad lakes. Always, high, grey peaks towered over them on either side. Later, there were no trees Shale and boulders stretched right down to the road. Except for a few cottages and the monastery of Beddgelert they saw no sign of life. Joslin and Gyll came from gentle landscapes in Suffolk and the Cotentin and these huge mountains awed and oppressed them. To Joslin it seemed as though this was his last barrier, even though the road was easy. Today was an image of his whole quest: dangerous peaks and precipices poised over him while he followed a narrow path between.

In the afternoon, they left the mountains and saw green, fertile land ahead. To find a farm near the road was a blessed relief. They bought rough cheese and drank water from the well. Then they faced the last miles to Ynis Mon, through more rolling country with the road always dropping down towards the sea.

Now they talked. "I dreamt of James Lamb last night," said Joslin.

"Forget James Lamb," Gyll replied. "Think of the good dream you had in Bala. What does that tell you?"

"It says that I knew my mother once. She cared for me and sang lullabies. I saw her as if I was a baby, but I also watched her through my eyes of today and I know that she was beautiful. She sang to me in a castle. I saw a hall and banners on the walls, like those in Stovenham or the count's castle at Treauville."

"Then surely you must have been in the count's castle," said Gyll.

"How could I be? My dream told me that I was in the boat afterwards, going to France, and my mother wasn't there."

"But you don't know if the voyage came before the castle."

"I know it didn't," said Joslin. "These may be dreams, but they're also memories which have lurked hidden in my mind since I was a baby My mother looked after me in a castle, then I went on the voyage with my father. The order is right. I feel it in my bones."

"If you lived in a castle where you were a baby, then perhaps you were born in one."

"Where could it have been but in the count's castle? But if it was, where was I sailing to?"

An hour later, they saw the keep of Caernarfon castle ahead. "We're nearly there," said Gyll. But Joslin felt no swell of joy at the sight. Those solid grey walls and towers and the huge stone keep gave him the usual shiver. "I know I wasn't born in *that* castle," he said.

"Don't worry. We won't be noticed," said Gyll.

"Even so, I'd like to keep away," Joslin replied.

They kept going until they were close to the sea, which Joslin had not seen since he walked from *The Merchant of Orwell* so long ago on the other side of the country. Ynis Mon, Anglesey, lay a mile across the strait. He frowned at the sight. "It looks a long way off," he said. "And the tide's out. There won't be any boats and we daren't take the horses across the sand. There may be quicksands and then, if we managed to get to the other side, great dunes to cross. The horses would never make it. We won't be there tonight."

"We will," Gyll answered confidently. "Look out to your left. There's the open sea. This must be the furthest edge of Anglesey. We'll go along the shore the other way. The straits between here and the island will get narrower. Remember the innkeeper. If you don't like the look of the castle, go somewhere else to find a boat to cross in."

She led him away through Caernarfon, under the castle's brooding shadow. Nobody took a second glance at them and soon they were making their way eastwards along the coast, watching the straits separating mainland and island become narrower, seeing boats cross between the two and at last, at Y Felinheli, finding a man by the shore with a ferry-boat big enough to take their horses.

The ferryman spoke Welsh. He seemed more hostile than anyone they had yet met as Joslin tried to make himself understood in English. He pointed to the island, to the boat, themselves, the horses, produced money, all to no avail. Before he tried the Breton which had worked for him previously, he spoke in French. At once the boatman smiled, helped them lead the horses on board and started to pole them across the Menai Strait.

"I don't believe he can speak French," Joslin muttered.

"I think it's just that you spoke something that wasn't English," Gyll replied.

The sea was calm and the clouds were breaking. A red setting sun lifted their hearts. The boatman never spoke. Joslin and Gyll calmed the horses and listened to the ripple and slap of water. The island came nearer and Joslin's heart beat faster. The ferryman avoided a grey expanse of mud and sand, the prow of the boat grounded on the far shore and they led the horses off. When Joslin felt hard land under his feet again, he was filled with extraordinary happiness. He held out coins to the boatman, who picked through them and took what he must have regarded as his proper fee. Joslin smiled, clapped him on the shoulder, said, "*Merci mille fois, mon ami,*" and gave him the same amount over again. The boatman looked at him without thanks. But his satisfied expression was answer enough for Joslin as he stood on the shore fingering Guillaume's locket, knowing with a sudden thrill that soon he might find out what had so tantalizingly rattled inside it since last September.

Gyll spoke. "St Ursula's shrine?" It sounded like a question.

Perhaps the boatman knew more English than he had let on. He pointed inland and said one word. "Aberffraw."

19

"Aberffraw?" Joslin repeated.

"Yes," said the ferryman. They stared at him. "I can speak English when I choose," he said. He put the money into a bag and laid it in the bows of the boat. "With you, I choose to."

"What is Aberffraw?" asked Gyll.

"Aberffraw is a goodly town and harbour, though the sand has spoilt the bay by its side. But most of all it was the seat of the princes of Gwynedd. That's important to Welshmen who sigh for the old days, when we had our own Prince of Wales." He looked at Gyll and said, "One day the English will be gone. We'll have our true Welsh prince again and his name will be Owain. What do you think of that, my lady?"

"I don't have to like everything my countrymen do," Gyll murmured. "You should have your princes back."

The ferryman seemed satisfied. But Joslin recalled the night in Sycharth, what Gruffydd had said and what Guillaume's errand had been all those years ago. What was the name Gruffydd mentioned?

"Will that prince be Owain Lawgoch?" he asked. "He's in France getting an army ready now, I'm told."

"Well, you should know, being French," said the ferryman "And may God be with him, because if he comes to Wales I'll join him, and so will most round here."

Joslin was troubled. What else did Gruffydd say? Owain Lawgoch gave Guillaume a letter to find what support he might hope for and James Lamb said Guillaume had not carried out his task. He remembered James Lamb at the stone circle – the dagger now lost in the waterfall was "given on trust" for "a job that was never done".

What if James Lamb spoke true? It left a bitter taste, to think that if it weren't for Guillaume the Welsh might have driven the English out by now, and Prince Owain of Wales might be ruling his own land from Aberffraw. There was more to this quest than a simple search for a missing mother.

"How far is Aberffraw?" asked Gyll. "Will we get there tonight?"

"I wouldn't even try," the ferryman answered. "You've got a long way to go, and if you get lost in the marshes and bogs round Malltraeth then you'll never see Aberffraw, and perhaps not anything else ever again."

"Then what can we do?" she said.

"Take the road inland to Llandaniel," he answered. "You'll find somewhere to stay if you tell them that Gwion the ferryman sent you."

"Thank you, Gwion," said Joslin. They mounted their horses and were away.

Gwion watched them go. He didn't think they were pilgrims to St Ursula's shrine, and he wondered what their real purpose was. He'd worked this ferry for many years, and learned much that would surprise his passengers, through observation and careful listening.

A young French minstrel and his lady. They reminded him of something his long-dead uncle, who had the ferry at Caernarfon, once told him. He tried to recall it – and when he did, he had a feeling that, sooner or later, someone would come that way looking for them. Well, he liked them, for all that the girl was English, and besides, the French boy had given twice the usual fare. So anyone asking questions would get short shrift from him. Especially if their voices sounded English.

Gwion was right. Mentioning his name got them lodging in Llandaniel and next morning they were heading westwards to the coast. The land was flat and rocky, but great tracts were bright with yellowing corn. By mid-morning they came to Newborough. Towards the sea was a forest: between its dark trees and Newborough were ruins. The man they bought food from told them they were the ruins of Rhosyr, once a palace belonging to the princes of Gwynedd, not as fine as Aberffraw, but important nevertheless. An hour later they saw what Gwion had meant about the marshes of Malltraeth. They would have been lost in that expanse of mud flats and shallow water with no visible track across them. The River Cefni wound through with never a ford or a bridge.

To their left was a large bay. The tide was nearly out, leaving great tracts of sand. They followed a path like a tightrope which disappeared altogether when they had to ford the Cefni. But when this obstacle was over, and the horses shook themselves free of water and mud, a firm track stretched ahead through open country and past sand dunes. Soon they came to Aberffraw, seat of the House of Gwynedd, and nearby, the object of their journey – St Ursula's shrine.

First they saw the harbour, where fishing boats clung to the quay with only the channel of the River Ffraw to float in now the tide had gone out. Beyond, larger boats fit for the open sea were moored. Next was the bustling little town, the fish-market, the rope-makers busy binding marram grass from the dunes into strong cable. Beyond were the ruins of the great house of Gwynedd, and the royal courthouse, and, nearby, the ancient church. Where was there a shrine?

Who to ask? The priest. They found him praying in front of the altar. "St Ursula's shrine?" he said. "Not in the town. What anchoress wanting to free herself of the world to be with God would stay in such a noisy place?"

"Anchoress?" asked Joslin.

"Of course, my son. Shrines have guardians, keepers. These guardians dedicate their lives to the shrines and their saints. St Ursula was a woman, so her shrine's guardian is a woman, an anchoress. She has shut herself away from the world of men and women, except for sincere pilgrims. She dedicates her life to her saint. She is dead to all that happened to her before, she has left behind all sins, all desires, all matters of the fallen human world. She has renounced her old name. Now she is called Dwynwen. Do not ask me what her name was before. Even if I knew I would not say, because her old life is dead. She lives only for God and the saint and seeks to be at one with them. That is an anchoress."

Joslin felt uneasy. If the priest was talking about his mother, then his quest would not end the way he wanted it to. If his mother had removed herself from the world, then she must have had good reason. If she was happy, then he would be happy for her. But she would not be the mother he had come so far to find.

"If the shrine isn't in the town, where is it?" asked Gyll.

"You walk north along the river," said the priest. "Soon after you leave the town, the river bends sharply to your right, then back on itself again. But at the point of this first right turn, you'll see a stream flowing straight ahead of you. Leave the river and follow this stream for half a mile. Another stream flows into it, again from the right. Follow this stream until you come to a rock on the left bank. You will see where the stream starts, from a spring between rocks on the side of the hill. Next to the spring is a cave and in it is a stone altar with a candle burning, shielded from the wind by more stones. Next to the cave is a stone hovel with a turf roof. That is the anchoress's cell."

"Why St Ursula?" asked Gyll. "She has nothing to do with Wales."

"No," said the priest. "And I cannot tell you everything because I have not long been here. My predecessor, old Rhodri, was here when the shrine was set up. Now he is dead, and much of what happened has died with him. I do know that nineteen years ago a great gift and blessing came to Aberffraw. Relics of the saint were brought here, and the shrine was made to keep them and be a place of pilgrimage. The bishop himself came to bless it. So it is a holy place and no wicked men dare go near, even though a woman stays there undefended and alone."

At last Joslin found his voice. "I have come many miles to see the shrine of St Ursula, and this is not what I expected to find."

"Then I might ask what it was you did expect?" said the priest.

Joslin said nothing. Gyll spoke for him. "Can we go there?"

"Of course you can go there. That is what shrines are for. But I suggest you wait until morning, to give you time to prepare your minds for the visit. You'll find an inn in the High Street which will give you rest for the night, but take no strong drink, be sparing with food and pray that your visit will grant all you expect from it."

They thanked him, left the church, found the inn and entered. At once, the conversation died. Every eye turned towards them. Joslin was sure he heard indrawn breaths of surprise. The innkeeper spoke to them in English. Yes, he could give them lodging, yes, he would give them water, though he'd rather they paid money for his good ale.

"We're going to the shrine tomorrow," said Joslin.

"Ah," said the innkeeper. "Devotees of St Ursula, are you?"

"No," Joslin replied. "I've come on a long journey and the shrine is my destination. It is the anchoress I want to see."

Gyll whispered in his ear. "You're telling him too much."

"No one here will take kindly to Dwynwen being upset," the innkeeper said. "She's a good woman, and if it's about her life before she came to the shrine, I'd advise you to ask nothing."

Joslin was aware that other men had risen and were standing round him, almost threateningly. "It was a long time ago, and I say sleeping dogs should be let lie," said one.

"Come away, Joslin," urged Gyll.

He shook her off. He was becoming annoyed. "I've not come this far to let sleeping dogs lie," he shouted. "I'm Joslin, son of Guillaume, who came here nineteen years ago. Now he's dead, foully murdered, and I'm looking for my mother. The end of my search is at the shrine."

"Calm down, son," said the innkeeper. "And you lot – " he gestured towards the men – "just go back to your places and drink your ale." He turned back to Joslin. "There's nothing to tell you, lad," he said. "Nobody here knows any more than you do. I reckon going to the shrine won't be the end of your search, but the beginning."

They were up early and on their way, following the priest's instructions. Joslin felt strange. Here he was, perhaps about to end his long search, yet unhappy. He might meet his mother at last and know who she was – but she would be barred to him, living a different life. He had never considered this, and now he realized how stupid he had been. If the blessed St Ursula was his goal, it was likely that his mother would be a nun or anchoress, making her dead to everything that had gone before. Another disturbing thought dawned. He might find his mother – but James Lamb had said that he would also find "proof" that Guillaume wasn't his father.

They found the bend in the river and followed the stream ahead, then the next stream flowing from the right until they came to the rock. Joslin's heart was beating fast.

"Listen," said Gyll. Though there were few trees, the air was loud with birdsong. "This is a good place."

They turned to where the land rose in a little hill with a close horizon. The stream tinkled down it, a sparkling, chuckling rill, from where the spring bubbled out of a clump of rocks. In the hill was a cave, dug out of the soil and shored up with rocks. Inside, as the priest had said, was a stone altar and on it, shaded by more stones, a candle burned.

Except for the gushing spring and birdsong, it was very quiet. They dropped to their knees. Joslin tried to pray but instead said out loud, "What have I done all this for?"

A voice cried, "Who comes to this shrine?" A woman approached, very thin, with a lined and weatherbeaten face. Yet Joslin had a feeling she was not old – certainly no more so than Guillaume when he died. "What is your business?" she said.

"We come as pilgrims," said Gyll.

"No," said Joslin. "We are more than that."

This was the moment. No matter what disappointment it would bring him, this was what he had to do. He took the locket from round his neck and handed it to her. "Can you unlock this?" he said.

She took it and examined it. Then she looked at him, a long, searching look. She went to the altar. From behind the candle, she took a small, worn, leather bag. She reached inside with bony fingers and took out a tiny key. She slipped the key into the keyhole, turned it and the locket opened. Out of it she took what looked like a tiny stick. She felt inside the leather bag again and this time took out another stick.

She fitted them together and held out what she had made with them. Now Joslin saw that it was not stick but bone. The two pieces fitted together perfectly to make a human knuckle-joint. From France, through England and, at last, to the saint's shrine, he had carried half of – "The holy relic of St Ursula," the woman said. "For so long in two parts: now at last joined up. Pilgrims can venerate the whole relic now."

She put the complete knuckle back in the leather bag and handed Joslin the empty locket. Then she looked at him and said, "Joslin."

20

"Yes," said Joslin. No more.

"At last," the anchoress said. "Sometimes I have longed for this day and sometimes I have dreaded it. Where is Guillaume?"

"Guillaume is dead," Joslin answered. "He told me there was only one key to the locket and it belongs to my mother."

The anchoress inclined her head and was silent, her lips moving as if in prayer. Then she murmured, "Only death could keep Guillaume away. God rest him." Joslin waited for her to say more. After an age, she spoke again. All she said was, "Did Guillaume tell you his story?"

"No," Joslin answered. "He said nothing until he was dying."

"Then I must tell you." Again she waited, gathering up her thoughts. At last she said, "Guillaume taught me many things. One of them was his minstrel's art of telling stories to all who would listen. I see from your harp that it is your art as well. I will tell this story as you and Guillaume would tell it. I shall not say 'I', because that will make it mere memory, and memory is faulty, too bound up with the teller. You want to know if I am your mother. To tell you now would awaken grief which I thought I had forgotten. Perhaps if I go as far as I can with those events as if they were in an old ballad, they may seem to have happened to someone else, not me. Then I might bring myself to answer your question."

She led them to her stone hovel. Though the entrance was open to the air, it was dark and dry inside. The floor was covered with clean rushes. In one corner was a rush mattress with sheepskins on it. By the mattress stood a candle: this she lit as they entered. Opposite was a little wooden crucifix hanging on the wall. On the floor beside the mattress were two round, smooth boulders: the anchoress motioned Joslin and Gyll to sit on them.

"Now I'll begin," said the anchoress. "Listen well. There was once a young girl who men said was the most beautiful woman in Wales. Her name was Rhiannon. She was the niece of Gruffydd Fychan, descendant of great princes, and since her mother had died and her father had been killed in battle, she was his ward as well. She lived at Sycharth in perfect happiness. Gruffydd loved Rhiannon as his own daughter, for as yet he had no children of his own, though soon afterwards a son was born, named Owain. Sometimes Gryfydd said that one day she should be mother to a new line of great Welsh princes.

"But many men looked at Rhiannon with desire in their hearts – and not just for her beauty. If a Welshman married her, he would unite his family

160

with one of the last Welsh dynasties, and great would be his power and influence in his own land. But if an Englishman married her – why, then there would be a bond tying the two lands even tighter together, and bringing favour in the sight of the king himself. Which would Gruffydd prefer? He would love his country to be free of the English. But he was also a realist and knew the English would always be there. They had been merciless in the past and could be merciless again, and he wanted no ruin to fall on his people.

"So when a kinsman of the Earl of March came calling, Gruffydd did nothing to stop him, though partly he regretted it. The Earl of March was the greatest English noble on the Welsh Marches and his word was law for many miles beyond his home at Chirk. For Sir Edmund Fitzgrace to marry Rhiannon of the House of Powys and thus unite the families might mean peace in Wales for ever. So it was decided. Rhiannon would be betrothed to Edmund and soon the great wedding would take place.

"Then, one night, there was a new arrival at Sycharth. Out of the dark came a man who had made a long journey. A mysterious stranger with news for Gruffydd. Gruffydd heard the news and his heart was troubled. Far away in France, there was a man of Gwynedd. He led a band of fugitive Welshmen who wanted to come back, drive the English away and set their leader up as the new, true Prince of Wales.

"Well, what was Gruffydd to do? Join with this man, Owain Lawgoch? His country might be free again, but he would have to do homage to a rival

Welsh family. Rhiannon's marriage would not take place, and there would be new enmity between Gruffydd and the Earl of March. Besides, could he trust the messenger?

"He was sure Edmund knew him, though Edmund said nothing. The man's name was James Lamb –"

"And he had a sallow, pockmarked face and a twisted lip," Joslin interrupted.

"A sallow face, yes, but no pockmarks and no twisted lip. James Lamb said that the news he brought would soon be shown as true. Another stranger would come to Sycharth with proof that Owain Lawgoch plotted to come to Wales. So Gruffydd told James Lamb he could stay as an honoured guest until his news was proved – and if it was true, then he could stay for as long as he liked. But if he was lying, then he would be a very sorry man.

"But James Lamb seemed sure that he was right, and it was now that Lady Rhiannon and her maidservant Olwen saw more of him. He haunted them: he followed them wherever they went, for he was soon besotted with Rhiannon, even though he knew that she was betrothed to Edmund. But Rhiannon would not look at him. Nobody told Gruffydd, for they knew the bargain he had made with James, but many hoped that no one would come with news of Owain Lawgoch, so that James would suffer the fate they thought he deserved.

"Then, one night, the expected visitor arrived. For the first time, Rhiannon and Olwen saw Guillaume de Lay, the minstrel. Gruffydd welcomed him and asked him to sing. Oh, how this Frenchman sang. No one had heard the like before. Who could forget that sweet, true voice and the harp like a gentle waterfall? Who could not be moved by that comely face and those gentle, smiling eyes? Rhiannon especially: at once the thought of Edmund was hateful to her. The minstrel Guillaume, whether high-born or low, whether French, Welsh or English, whether with a life of ease or hard travel to offer, was the man for her. She felt it like a bolt of lightning on the mountains above Sycharth.

"When the playing was over, she told her maidservant Olwen what she felt and Olwen was troubled. She urged her mistress to forget the minstrel, because no love could be certain in a mere instant and the wrath of Gruffydd and Edmund together would be dreadful. But Rhiannon would have none of it. 'I must go with him, Olwen,' she said. 'We must leave tonight, because once my love is known then Guillaume's life may be in danger. You must stay here. I'll have no need of servants and it would be best if you can say you knew nothing of my intention.'

"Meanwhile, Guillaume was summoned to Gruffydd's solar by Rhys, his servant, and there he showed the proof he had brought Now Gruffydd was troubled, for when he saw the seal of the House of Gwynedd he knew that both James and Guillaume spoke true. If he held Guillaume prisoner and destroyed the letter and the seal of Gwynedd, then if the truth became known he would be hated by all Welshmen. But if he helped raise an army to join Owain, then at best he would see a rival prince over all Wales; at worse he would plunge Wales into new wars, and the English would surely destroy his land for ever. What was he to do?

"He resolved to let Guillaume carry on with his mission and take Owain's letter to other Welsh houses. That way, he would know what his countrymen thought. If they were in support, he would join. If they rejected it, then he would reject it as well. So he told Guillaume he could leave and carry on with the task Owain Lawgoch had given him – but meanwhile he was an honoured guest until such time as he was rested from his long journey.

"But James Lamb had different ideas. He knew that if he could get hold of that letter he would have great power, either with the Welsh or with the English, whoever would give him the greatest reward. Besides, he saw how Guillaume and Rhiannon looked at each other. He saw Edmund's fury as well. He felt the bitter taste of his own jealousy. He knew Guillaume was his enemy, both because he had the letter and because Rhiannon might love him.

"While everyone else in the hall had eyes only for Guillaume, Olwen had eyes only for James. She was a young and lovely lady, though not as lovely as Rhiannon, and many men among the servants lusted after her. But she would have none of them, just as she would let no men of high rank have their way with her either. But when she saw James, she knew her real and only love was here. She wondered how she could know him better and somehow put him in her debt. When she heard Rhiannon's plans, she thought her chance had come. With Rhiannon gone, she would have James to herself. So she had to help her mistress. How would she do it?

"Rhys, the servant, was a true Welshman. He wanted his countrymen to know about Owain Lawgoch's call to arms. Like all good servants, he was loyal to Gruffydd, his master, and when he knew that Gruffydd wanted Guillaume to carry on with his journey he was pleased. But he was no fool. He distrusted James Lamb. He knew what a prize that letter would be to anyone who didn't care how he used it. Guillaume had to be got away in case Lamb reached him first. Rhys had seen how Rhiannon and Guillaume looked at each other. Rhys was horrified that a Welsh girl should be made to marry a man as English as Edmund Fitzgrace. He made up his mind. He would help Rhiannon and Guillaume escape.

"There was one matter which Rhys kept safe within himself. He loved Olwen. Olwen had no idea what he felt. But everyone else knew, by Rhys's covert little glances and sighs as she walked past. They saw the strong, bearded man with a cast in one eye reduced to trembling by this dark-haired girl and they were sad, for they knew Olwen would never look twice at him. Nevertheless, Rhys saw a chance to make her think well of him. He reasoned that Rhiannon would tell Olwen of her wish. If he, Rhys, could make it happen, then Olwen might love him out of gratitude.

"Rhys found her in the servants' hall and took her to one side where no one could hear. 'Olwen,' he said, 'I have a question to ask. Do you know how much your mistress hates her Englishman? Did you see the way she and the Frenchman looked at each other?'

"'I did,' Olwen answered. 'I fear for them both.'

"'Then we must help her, you and I,' said Rhys. 'The minstrel is in danger. He must get away from here tonight and we must make sure that Rhiannon goes with him.'

"'Very well,' said Olwen. 'I'll do it for my mistress, because I know she desires it so much.'

"So together they worked out how Rhiannon would escape with Guillaume. When their plans were ready, Rhys said, 'Now I will leave you. I'll help Guillaume. You must see to your mistress. Everything must be done as we agreed. Be quiet and careful.' Soon Guillaume was waiting with his horse behind the dovecote, while Rhiannon, hooded so nobody would recognize her, waited where the moat was shallow.

"Meanwhile, James was also thinking. He had to get the letter off Guillaume. By now, Guillaume would be asleep in the minstrels' loft. James could move silently and thieve so that nobody would know they had been robbed. He climbed into the loft to search Guillaume's clothes and belongings. But when he looked inside, he saw that Guillaume wasn't there. Not were any of his belongings. Only Y Bergam the bard lay snoring in the straw. Where could Guillaume be?

"He realised at once – Guillaume had escaped. James wanted to know three things. Had Rhiannon gone with him? Who had helped him? Would Gruffydd hunt him down when he found out? He didn't want that – he wanted Guillaume for himself. The best way to know all this was to raise the alarm. So that is what he did.

"When the alarm was over and everyone had gone back to their beds, he considered what he now knew. First, as he suspected, Rhys had helped Guillaume. Second, Rhiannon had not gone with him. Olwen said she slept soundly. Third, there would be no chase after Guillaume.

"He was about to go to his bed when he thought – *How did he know Rhiannon had not gone? Why hadn't she come outside with the others when the alarm was raised?* He only had Rhys's word that Olwen said she was asleep.

"He knew how to find out. He went to a small chamber next to Rhiannon's, knocked on the door and softly called, 'Olwen.'

"Meanwhile, Rhiannon and Guillaume rode on into the night. And when morning came, James Lamb was nowhere to be found and Olwen was crying in her grief."

21

Joslin shifted uncomfortably on his stone. He saw Gyll looking hard at the anchoress, as if trying to haul something out of the woman's mind, some statement more revealing than this story.

But what could be more revealing? Rhiannon *must* be his mother. She could surely never love a man so devious as James Lamb. What a relief that he had disappeared over the edge at the waterfall of Pystyll Rhaedr. His footsteps would not dog them now

The anchoress continued in her low, urgent voice. As she spoke, Joslin felt he might well get used to the idea of this woman with the lined, gaunt, nut-brown face as his mother.

"Rhiannon and Guillaume rode through the misty darkness for many miles. 'My dear, we must get far away before morning,' said Rhiannon. 'When daylight comes and they know we're gone, they'll hunt us, and it would not go well with us if we were caught.'

"'Rhiannon,' answered Guillaume. "I know I'm dreaming. It's not possible that I could see the lady of my dreams for the first time in my life this very evening, knowing that I could only love her from afar, and yet now before the sun is up I'm running away with her like some callow and innocent boy eloping with his girl.'

"'You aren't dreaming, my dearest Guillaume,' Rhiannon answered. 'We loved each other at once – as, in the old story, Pwll, Prince of Dyfed and *his* Rhiannon loved each other at first sight, and lived in perfect amity all their lives, though disasters beset them round about. Nothing matters now except that we should be together.'

"But Guillaume was troubled. As he rode the horse that Owain Lawgoch himself gave him, he felt guilt rising up. 'Rhiannon, there's something else, and it matters much,' he said. 'I have a task placed on me by a man I respect and fear. There is a message, Owain Lawgoch's call to arms, that I must deliver to all the strongest men in Wales. I promised Owain, and Gruffydd wants me to do it despite his doubts.'

"'Guillaume, if we go looking for all the strongest men in Wales, we'll surely be taken and given back to the very people I'm running from,' Rhiannon replied. 'I won't marry Edmund. I love *you*, we're together and that is all that matters.'

"Guillaume did not answer. He was uneasy about his mission. But then dawn broke, the mists cleared, the sun rose, Rhiannon took her hood from her face and turned to look at Guillaume. His heart turned over and he knew that nothing else in the whole world mattered."

The anchoress's voice changed and Joslin knew the story was taking a bad turn: it was a change in tone that he often used himself.

"But Rhiannon and Guillaume were not the only riders through the mountains. When James knocked on Olwen's door and softly called 'Olwen' the maidservant recognized his voice. She opened the door with wildly beating heart. Her eyes were alight with expectancy and suddenly James Lamb realized what he had not noticed before – this woman loved him. Of course. Now he had the key to everything. He murmured false words of love to her and she listened, lips parted in ecstasy. Then he said, 'Olwen, I know Rhiannon has escaped with the minstrel. Where are they going? You'll tell me, your true love who has come to you in the night, won't you?'

"'I don't know,' Olwen murmured. 'I wish I did. I would do anything, tell you anything, if it would please you.'"

"'But your mistress must have said something,' said James. 'Was there no hint that you can remember?'"

"'Not on this night,' Olwen replied. 'But I have heard my mistress say that if Gruffydd had been descended from the princes of Gwynedd instead of Powys, and we lived at Aberffraw and not Sycharth, he would never have let her marry an Englishman.'"

" 'Gwynedd,' James said musingly. 'Aberffraw.' Then he said, 'Olwen, you've helped me very much. I thank you,' and turned to go. But Olwen reached out, clasped her hands round him and pulled him towards her bed. James Lamb, being but a man as other men are, let it happen, lay down with her and did not rise again until she was asleep with a smile of contentment on her face and dawn had nearly come. At last he rose, crept out of her room and out of Sycharth, took his horse and murmured again, 'Aberffraw. Of course.' Soon he was on their trail.

"There was murder in his heart now. He cared nothing for Olwen, however pleasant his hour with her had been. He wanted Rhiannon, but if she knew he intended to rob and kill Guillaume she would cast him away for ever. No, he must be far more subtle. As he rode, many plans came to his mind, but all of them he rejected – too obvious, too difficult, too dangerous to him. If only he could do something which would ruin Guillaume's life *and yet keep him alive so that he went through the misery of loss for many, many years.* Yes, that was what he had to do. But how was he to do it?""

Well, he had done it, thought Joslin – all those years Guillaume spent exiled from his wife, bound together only by a locket with a relic in it and memories kept secret until the very last moments. At least, he felt with guilty satisfaction, he had gained revenge for his father.

The anchoress went on. "Rhiannon and Guillaume rode on together, saying little, glorying in being with each other. Rhiannon said, 'I know you have a task to perform and I know, because I'm Welsh, how important it is that you do it. You made a promise and our people look for a new leader who will raise us up again. But what I said is still true. We would be taken and given back at once. There's just one place where we might be safe. There your message would be received with joy, and those who read it would fight to the death to make sure that I would not be sent back to marry Edmund.'

"'Where is that?' Guillaume asked.

"'Aberffraw, in Ynys Mon, or Anglesey as the English say,' Rhiannon replied. 'Once the seat of the Princes of Gwynedd, but fallen now on hard times. The great palace was destroyed years ago. With Edward's castles at Beaumaris and Caernarfon to keep watch and English justices and coroners to run the island, there's little hope for its rise again in Anglesey. The House of Gwynedd led the last battles against Edward and they paid dearly for them. You'll carry out your promise to Owain because the people of Aberffraw will receive your letter gladly. You can be sure that if there's a chance to raise arms against King Edward given them by one of their own, however far away he is, then the people of Aberffraw and all those who remember the great days of Llewellyn and Dafydd will take it.'

"'To Aberffraw, then,' said Guillaume.

"So on they went, through the mountains to Ffestiniog and the Pass of Aberglaslyn, with the great peak of Mynydd Mawr to their left and the even greater peak of Yr Wyddfia to their right, carrying on by day and by night, never stopping near the haunts of men but resting under trees and rocks, eating berries and drinking water from the streams, keeping on though they were wet through with mist and rain, cold and shivering in the night, sleeping in the saddle while their horses wandered and staggered with weariness.

"And James Lamb followed, out of sight but watching, watching.

"At last the mountains were gone and they came to the fertile lands leading down to Menai. They were grieved to see such ruin, so many deserted houses, so many untilled fields, because here the plague had left a terrible mark. And then before them stood Caernarfon castle, with its forbidding stone towers, the very mark of the English. Sudden fear seized Rhiannon. She gripped Guillaume's arm and said, "I'm sorry, my love. We have come all this way to the home of the oppressor. Your life would be worth nothing, and nor would my love or my freedom, if we are seen here.'

"'Be strong, Rhiannon,' Guillaume answered. 'We'll go to the shore and find a ferryman to take us to the island, as if it is our right and our regular custom. Nobody will notice us if we go confidently through. Walk straight, with your head held high and a spring in your step and you'll never be doubted. I've come a long way from France and I never felt afraid until I crossed Offa's Dyke to come into Wales, but I've not come this far to be taken now. We have our love and the happiness that waits ahead to carry us through. Everybody will see that and rejoice for us, so no one will hinder us as we pass.'

My father was braver than I was, thought Joslin.

"But as they found a ferryman willing to take them and they slipped across the Menai Straits, James Lamb was hurrying down to the shore and watching them go. He knew what would happen. They were looking for a once-royal family, still smarting with deprivation, who would come to their aid and give them help. But they would find, by the ruins of a palace, a poor village in which a few bondmen tried to scratch a living and pay their rents to English landlords, as they still mourned the so-recent dead from the great plague. 'You would have done better to stay where you were,' he said to himself."

The anchoress paused. "Go on," said Joslin.

"It was evening when they landed at Abermenai," she said. "As soon as they stepped on the sandy shore they felt safe. They were also very tired. 'Where is the nearest place to eat and sleep?' Rhiannon asked the ferryman. 'Newborough,' was the reply. 'It's an English town. But close by are the ruins of Cae Llys at Rhosyr, a palace of the princes of Gwynedd like Aberffraw. Their memory lives on in Newborough. You'll rest easy.'

"So they came to Newborough, where sand comes up from the sea and merges with dark forests close to the ruins of Rhosyr. They found an inn and rested for the night.

"Meanwhile, back at Caernarfon, the ferryman found another fare waiting. He took the passenger with a bad grace, because he knew by the voice what sort of man it was who commanded him. 'On your last crossing you carried two travellers, a man and a woman.' ,this man said as if he was a lord talking to a serf. 'Where did they go after they left you?' The ferryman replied, 'I never asked: it isn't my business.' Then he had an idea and added, 'But the man said to the lady that they should ride fast through the night to Holyhead and take ship to Ireland.'

"'Ireland,' James Lamb repeated and did not seem to think the ferryman had lied to him. 'Ireland. Yes. It's possible.'

"Then he spurred his horse on and disappeared into the dusk, while the ferryman murmured to himself, 'I don't know who you two young people are, but may God preserve you from that man.'

"Next morning, Rhiannon and Guillaume came to Aberffraw. It was as the ferryman said – a ruined place, deserted court-house and tumbledown houses lived in by a few families still recovering from the plague.

"They rode down the street and thought the town was empty except for a few pigs, chickens and thin, spiritless dogs. 'Where are the folk?' asked Guillaume. Rhiannon said, 'If I lived here, and I saw riders on horseback, I'd hide because I'd fear them.' Guillaume answered, 'If I were a Welshman I'd think that riders on horseback were English, so I'd come out to kill them.' They got off the horses and Guillaume, as so often when in doubt, took his harp and started to play and sing. Gradually, first one woman, then another, then another emerged to listen and children followed. No men. Guillaume finished his song. Then Rhiannon spoke in Welsh, long and passionate. The women burst out in excited answer. They took Guillaume and Rhiannon into a cottage, sat them down and brought bowls of thin broth, while the children led the horses to shelter with the other animals.

"'What did you say to them?" Guillaume asked. Rhiannon answered, 'I said I was a Welsh woman escaping from an English lord who wants to marry me though I hate him. You are my only true love, a minstrel whose songs charm birds out of trees. The English want to kill you because you are French and brought a message from Owain Lawgoch. We came here to seek protection from people who will not forget the true princes of Gwynedd and the last battles of Llewellyn and Dafydd against the English. I said our pursuers may be close behind.'

"'How did they answer?' said Guillaume.

"'When their menfolk come in from the fishing boats they will decide what to do,' Rhiannon replied. 'But Mared, wife to Meic, the chief man of the town, says that to put ourselves beyond the clutches of the English we should marry. Here and now.'"

"''Here and now?' Guillaume repeated wonderingly. Then, 'Why not, since we *will* marry one day. Neither James nor Edmund could touch us then. Is there a priest in Aberffraw? If he's near, we'll do it.'

"''Oh, yes,' Rhiannon answered. 'A priest, and a church as well.' "

Joslin had been holding his breath, but now he let it out in a long sigh. "So they married?" he said.

"Yes," the anchoress replied. "The old priest Rhodri was found and they told him their story. 'I understand your plight,' he said. 'No matter what my bishop might say, I'll marry you here and now.' And he did.

"Back at Sycharth, Olwen was questioned by Gruffydd and Edmund. She was so frightened that she nearly blurted everything out, but she saw Rhys glaring at her. Besides, she felt humiliated because

James Lamb had taken what he wanted from her and left without a word. Some things she would tell nobody. She thought hard about what to do but found no answer. Then, that evening, there was again a knock at her door. There stood Rhys, hot and sweating. 'Let me in,' he said.

"'I will not,' Olwen answered angrily.

"'You must, for both our sakes,' he pleaded. "'Olwen, we have come to a pretty pass. We're responsible for what Rhiannon has done and you can be sure that devil Lamb knows. If he comes back, it's all up with us. What are we to do?'

"But Olwen still had no answer. Her mind was spinning with anger at James's leaving and frustration at not being able to tell anyone.

"'I've done a terrible thing,' Rhys groaned. 'I cheated my master by helping them go. I did it for love of you. I thought you'd love a man who helped your mistress and the minstrel escape.'

" 'Never,' Olwen cried. 'I've given my love to a better man than you, and now he's gone I don't care what happens to you.' The words were out before she could stop them.

"'What better man?' said Rhys. Then he saw the answer in her eyes. 'I see how the land lies,' he said. 'You and I have a common interest, Olwen.'

"Olwen looked at his big, clumsy body, hairy, sweat-beaded face and his left eye with the cast in it and felt revulsion 'Maybe,' she answered. 'But that common interest won't lead to love.'

"'Perhaps in time . . .' Rhys began.

"'Never,' said Olwen. 'But, for now, we must help each other.'

"'Do you know where they've gone?' Rhys asked.

"Now a wicked serpent whispered into Olwen's ear and told her to cheat Rhys. 'No,' she said. 'Do you know where James Lamb went?'

'No,' Rhys answered.

'So Olwen kept to herself her certainty that they were gone to Aberffraw and that James had followed because she had told him to. She formed a new plan, which she *would* carry out, though it made her tremble.

"'Olwen,' said Rhys, 'we must go to Gruffydd and tell him that we think Rhiannon and Guillaume fled because James Lamb urged them to. We must say that we never trusted him. You'll say that after they'd gone you confessed to me that you knew of a plot to escape between James, Rhiannon and the minstrel. I'll say that I've brought you to our master as a good servant should and that you know you should have spoken earlier but were afraid. You must throw yourself on his mercy and crave forgiveness. That's all that we can do. Gruffydd will forgive you. It's Edmund you must look out for.'

"So they went together before Gruffydd. He listened and he did forgive her. He praised her for her loyalty to her mistress, but chided her for not realizing that her duty to him was greater. Rhys was happy. Gruffydd still thought well of him and Olwen would soon realize how much she owed him. Olwen too was happy, but she told nobody why.

"That night she prepared for a journey. She took her warmest cloak and oldest clothes. She also took a knife which Rhiannon once gave to her to protect herself from drunken serving men. Then she went out into the night and down to the stables. The stable lads were asleep on the straw. She found her own horse next to the stall which once held Rhiannon's and led it out of the stables. Then she jumped on its back, took the reins and was away, through the moat and then northwards, towards where she was sure Rhiannon would be. She felt the weight of the knife at her waist and imagined it plunged into the false heart of James. The thought gave her strength as her horse took her ever northwards.

"She rode through the night, following the same path as Rhiannon, Guillaume and, later, James. Like them, she kept on, not caring how tired she was, though next evening she stopped in Beddgelert. A solitary woman on a journey raised eyebrows there when people saw her, but the fierceness in her face made them flinch and this stopped unwelcome attention. She found a night's lodging, left early in the morning and next evening she was asking the ferryman at Caernarfon for a crossing.

"She said nothing as he poled his boat away from the shore. But he was a shrewd, far-seeing man who had taken many passengers across with strange errands, and he had a strong suspicion about this one. So he said, 'If I were to tell you that a young woman of our country, and a Frenchman with a harp, crossed in my boat not two days since, and they were followed by a man who boded ill for them, what would you say?'

"Olwen wondered whether this was a trick and did not answer. The ferryman said, 'Believe me, I am an honest man and wish only for the young couple's good. I feared this man.'

"So Olwen said, 'Then I would ask whether the young couple were bound for Aberffraw and whether this man has found them there.'

"The ferryman answered, 'Yes, the couple were bound for Aberffraw, but as to whether the man found them, I can't say, because I tried to send him elsewhere. Somewhere far away. Ireland.'

" 'Did he go?' asked Olwen.

" 'Lady, how can I tell you that?'

"When they reached the other shore, the ferryman put Olwen on the road to Aberffraw and she left him, her heart pounding with fear because James Lamb might already be there. But when she came to the village and asked the first person she saw, she was taken to a cottage once lived in by a family dead of the plague, which had been made ready for the new bride and groom. Here she found Guillaume and Rhiannon. They were now man and wife, and the villagers had given them as great a feast as their meagre stocks would let them.

"When Olwen had got over her first happiness, she asked, 'But hasn't James Lamb been here?'

"Guillaume laughed. 'Why should we invite him to the wedding?'

"'Because he followed you. He landed on the island.'

"'Then where is he?'

"'The ferryman said he may have tricked him into going to Ireland.'

"'The ferryman must be right,' cried Guillaume. 'James Lamb has gone and he'll never come back. We're safe. Welcome, Olwen, and rejoice with us.'

"'Yes. Welcome, dearest Olwen,' said Rhiannon. 'Share in our joy.'

"But there was a doubt in Olwen's heart which stopped her rejoicing as she wanted to. At Sycharth, who knew how Rhys felt, deserted and cheated, with no idea how the plan he had himself first thought of was turning out?"

Joslin felt he had to interrupt. "Rhys has been murdered," he said. "He helped us get away from Sycharth and told us we must wait for him outside. I'm sure that if he could he would have let us know what happened all those years ago. We found his body. We knew we were in danger so we had to leave it there. We did not like doing that."

The anchoress received this news without answer.

"Is that the end of the story?" asked Gyll.

"No," replied the anchoress. Her voice was leaden. "But I can tell you no more."

"Why not?" cried Joslin.

The anchoress did not answer, but a look of pain crossed her face. "So Rhys is dead," she said.

"We don't know who killed him," Joslin replied. "It might have been Edmund. He was there in Sycharth."

"James Lamb killed him," said the anchoress. "I *know* it."

"James Lamb wasn't at Sycharth. He followed us, but we gave him the slip. It was chance that he found us again. And he died by chance."

"James Lamb is dead?" cried the anchoress as if Joslin had spoken the unbelievable. "It's not possible. He does nothing by chance."

181

"He did this time. He fell to his death. I thought I'd killed him but a priest told me I did not. He said that God decided James Lamb had done enough harm in the world and that was why he went over the edge."

For a moment the anchoress made no answer. Then she cried aloud: "If only that were true. It's Rhys I grieve for. He waited nearly twenty years, not knowing what had happened but uncomplaining like the good servant he was. And his reward has been death."

Then her face seemed to set itself in stone as if she would never speak again.

22

"Why can't you finish the story?" Joslin repeated.

At first the anchoress did not seem to hear. Then her face relaxed and she focused her eyes on him. "I'll tell you a little, because you've come a long way ," she said. "But soon I must stop because it will be too hard for me. They all lived in Aberffraw happy and contented. For all she was a high-born lady, Rhiannon worked with the women, while Guillaume went out each day with the fishermen. Meic and Mared took Olwen in to live with them. Each evening, Guillaume sang to the folk. Soon it was clear that Rhiannon was with child and great was the rejoicing. Olwen too was happy for them, but she had a secret of her own. She was with child as well, and who could the father be but James Lamb?"

Joslin felt cold. He could hear Lamb's voice: *"You'll find proof . . ."*

The anchoress stopped, head bowed, her hands clasped together in her lap. "I can say no more," she said.

"*Please,*" Joslin urged.

" I can say no more," she repeated. "I came out of the world because it was too grievous for me to stay in it. Some memories are so bitter that I will never be free of them. I cannot speak them and you must not ask me. You must be content with that."

"I'm sorry," Joslin replied. "I can't be content."

The anchoress was silent again. Joslin and Gyll waited. Gyll whispered, "Don't push her too far."

Then the anchoress said, "Leave me now. I knew I would have to say these things aloud one day. You have brought that day with you. Come back tomorrow. I shall spend the night in prayer, asking for strength to finish the story in the morning light. Now, go back to Aberffraw and be quick about it. You don't know who you may meet on the way."

"Who would harm us here?" Joslin insisted. "This is a place of friends."

"No place in this world has only friends in it. We must not anger the creatures of the night, for they surround us all the time. Go."

Joslin still hesitated. Gyll pulled him by the sleeve. "Come on, Joslin. We have to go now. You can't insist."

"Hear her, Joslin," said the anchoress. "You have the right partner there. Always hear her. She speaks true. Now go."

They walked slowly back, saying little. At the inn, they found a large man waiting, old but strong, with a gentle, weatherbeaten face.

"Ah," he said, looking at Joslin. "I see Guillaume in your eyes. I'm Meic, his friend. I'd know you anywhere, for all it's so long ago."

"Then you *do* remember," said Joslin eagerly. "I thought nobody here knew who I was."

"Oh, the older ones like me remember very well," Meic answered.

"Then can *you* tell us what happened?" Joslin burst out. "The anchoress won't say any more. She won't even say if she's my mother."

"I wish I could," Meic replied. "But it's not my place to. Not yet. Though I'll never forget Rhiannon or Guillaume or Olwen. Never, no matter what has happened since. Though that's little help to you."

"Why should you forget them?" Joslin asked. "The anchoress is still here."

"Joslin, Dwynwen has left the world we live in. She's dead to us and lives only for God."

"I know that," said Joslin. "But she still remembers."

Meic gripped Joslin's shoulder. "I know you've told people that Guillaume is dead. I'm deeply sorry, for him and for you. But I'm so pleased to see you here, and your lady as well. We'll do all we can for you both." Then Meic left the inn.

"Why won't anybody tell me what happened?" cried Joslin.

"Be patient," said Gyll softly. "I think they don't know enough to tell you. Perhaps the truth isn't what you've been hoping for."

Joslin remembered his sudden chill when the anchoress said that Olwen was with child. "Could Olwen be my mother?" he said.

Gyll did not answer directly. "Do you think she is?" she said.

For a moment, Joslin did not answer. Gill knew he was having bad thoughts.

185

At last he spoke. "If she is, then Lamb's my father and I couldn't bear that. But Meic thought I was Guillaume's son as soon as he saw me."

"Yet Lamb says he has proof that you aren't," said Gyll.

"Guillaume said the key to the locket belonged to my mother. Well, the anchoress had the key. I'll never forget when she took out the relic, looked at me and said 'Joslin'. So the anchoress must be my mother. What grief stops her finishing the story?" A look of horror crossed his face. "Gyll, there were two children, Rhiannon's and Olwen's. Which one am I? I have a terrible fear that James Lamb really is my father."

Meic did not leave the inn alone. He touched a few men on the arm as he went out. They followed him as he went round the village knocking on doors, and bringing more men out, until he had a band fifteen strong.

They went together down to the harbour. Below them, boats lay at anchor, bobbing on the water now it was high tide. Here, Meic spoke.

"'Friends, we are a good crew for a voyage and that's what I propose we make now. Many of you remember, and if you don't, your fathers will have told you, what happened here nineteen years ago when Rhiannon and Guillaume her minstrel came to Aberffraw, and Olwen followed Some of you know how we welcomed them here, we protected them, and then we lost them because we had no power to do any better. Well, I say we should try to do better for the sakes of these two young people. There's a voyage the men of this village have to make. I think most of you will know where that voyage will take us, but none of you know what will happen when we get there any more than I do. Perhaps we're going into danger – perhaps death. But I say that we have to try. It's our duty. We owe it to the minstrel Joslin and his lady after what we failed to do when Rhiannon, Guillaume and Olwen came to us all those years ago. Now, are you all with me?"

There was a murmur of assent. Then Meic said, "Go to your homes and tell your wives that you may be away for some days. Don't tell them about danger. Say that we shall come back soon enough, but whether our return brings good or ill is something we shall have to wait for God himself to make clear. They must say nothing to the minstrel about this until we return. Meet back here in an hour."

An hour later they boarded the *Newyddion Da,* a fine boat fit for long voyages. Soon they were poling it down the channel, past where the rocks began at Tywyn Du, until they came to the open sea. Here they hoisted the single sail, rounded the headland of Braich Lwyd and the rocky island of Carreg-y-trai and sailed westwards against the wind as dawn was breaking.

When Joslin slept, the dreams came in the familiar order. Firstly, a mother and a castle. He saw it more clearly now, like a real memory. The warmth of love from the woman who nursed him was not like a dream. It was part of his life that he had forgotten.

Then he was on the ship again and the storm woke him up.

At once the questions hammered in his head – *What is that great grief of the anchoress? Which of the two children was I?*

Outside, there was no storm. The day was fine. The sun shone, birds sang, a fresh breeze blew off the sea and they felt good on their way to the shrine. "I dreamt of my mother and the castle last night," he told Gyll. "But there are no castles round here except Caernarfon and Beaumaris and I can't see myself as a baby in either. And all the royal palaces on the island are in ruins, destroyed by the English."

"The answer will come," said Gyll.

They walked on, thinking of the anchoress's secret sorrow and hoping a night of prayer would have unlocked her tongue. They came to the second stream, followed it to the rock and listened for the birds of yesterday.

They listened in vain. There was no birdsong except for three black crows cawing as they flapped slowly overhead.

They came to the little hill. There was the spring, bubbling away as if nothing could ever happen. It seemed in some strange way to mock them. They were quiet, as if afraid to speak. The crows had perched on the rock, watching with hooded eyes.

Joslin and Gyll came to the cave, the shrine and the altar, on which the candle still burned. All seemed exactly as it should be. But silence lay on them like a stifling cloak.

"Something's wrong," said Gyll.

Joslin called softly. "Hello. We're here."

No answer. He called again, louder. Still no answer.

"She's still praying in her cell," he said. "We shouldn't interrupt."

Even so, they silently approached the hovel, listening for the mutters of prayers. They heard nothing. They stood outside, undecided.

"Should we look in?" said Gyll.

"Not if she's praying," Joslin answered.

They listened again. Complete silence. They looked at each other. A fearful realization was breaking on them.

Gyll grasped Joslin's hand. He squeezed it, took a deep breath and then they went forward together. They stopped at the entrance to the cell and looked in. The stones were where they were left last night, ready for them to sit on and listen. But there would be no listening done that day, or any other. Dwynwen was dead. She had been strangled. She was sprawled across her rush mattress, her head at an odd angle, her face purple, her tongue hanging out. The wooden crucifix that had been above her bed was now clasped in her hands. Joslin turned, threw his arms round Gyll and sobbed on her shoulder.

She let him cry until he calmed enough to say, tears streaming down his face, "My mother, my mother. I've come so far looking for her, and soon as I find her again I've lost her."

23

"We must do something," said Gyll.

Joslin had to climb out of a black pit before he could put his mind together and answer. He remembered what happened with bodies he had found before. "We need a coroner," he said.

"Who is he? Where do we find him?" said Gyll.

"Meic will know," said Joslin. But he didn't move. He was falling into the black hole again.

"We have to leave here," Gyll urged

"She might have been my mother," Joslin moaned again.

"Leave her!" Gyll cried.

At last, unwillingly, Joslin moved. They ran back to Aberffraw, to find that Meic and the strongest and best seafarers of the town were gone on a voyage and no one would say for how long. They looked for the priest: when they blurted out their news, he said, "Take me there."

They stumbled back to the shrine. The crows were gone: the silence was even more profound. The priest fells to his knees in front of Dwynwen's body with a cry of grief. Then he stood up, stepped back, took a deep breath and performed the rites for the dead. His voice rose and fell in the familiar Latin. Then he said, "We must get men from the town to bring her in with all reverence. I must send word to the bishop. He must bed told about this, because Dwynwen was a most holy woman."

"We'll never hear the end of her story now," said Joslin.

"There is a death-dealer in our midst," said the priest.

"The anchoress must have welcomed her murderer as a pilgrim," Gyll replied.

They walked away together. When they reached the broad river, Joslin said, "Father, why is the shrine in that place?"

"I do not rightly know," he answered. "I've only lately come here. It was set up in the time of my predecessor, Rhodri."

"But you told us that the shrine was made nineteen years ago, after the great blessing to Aberffraw of the saint's relic."

"I did."

"That was when Rhiannon and Guillaume came to Aberffraw."

"So I am told."

"Father, when he died, Guillaume gave me a locket with half of the relic in it. Dwynwen had the key to the locket, took out that half and fitted it to the other on the altar. That was how she knew I was Joslin. She had been waiting for me all these years."

The priest said nothing.

"Father, Guillaume said that the key belonged to my mother and that when I was in Wales I should look for the 'Blessed St Ursu...' But he died before he could finish. Well, I found the Blessed St Ursula and I gave the relic to the anchoress and the anchoress had the key. It must show that Dwynwen was my mother."

The priest still did not answer.

"And all this means I've come so far only to see my mother dead in front of me. I've seen murders enough these last months, but I never thought my own mother would be one of them."

At last, the priest spoke. "Joslin," he said, "soon I will give you comfort and you will be able to receive it. But remember, I am a priest. Dwynwen was a holy woman. I know nothing of her life before that and it is not my duty to ask. Besides, I was not here when Rhodri received the relic and when he told the bishop about it. It was then that the shrine was set up and consecrated."

"With my mother as anchoress?" Joslin said.

"As I understand it, you were not yet born," the priest replied. "Married, pregnant women cannot be anchoresses. Dwynwen may not have been the first to tend the shrine."

"Then she was the second," said Joslin. "Perhaps the first one died."

"I can't say. Have you considered that Dwynwen might not have been your mother?"

"She must have been. She had the key. She knew me. She knew Guillaume. She said, "Guillaume taught me many things.""

"I can't say," the priest repeated. "As anchoress, she named herself after Dwynwen, our own saint from Anglesey. Dwynwen of the Spring, we called her. I can't tell you what she was before and I'd never ask even those who might know, out of respect for her holy calling."

"But Father . . ." Joslin began.

"We must return to Aberffraw and find men to bring her back," said the priest.

When they came to the town, Joslin looked round at the cottages, innocent with the sun shining on their thatched roofs, and said, "Yes. There's a death-dealer here. I mean to find who it is."

"God will point his finger at the guilty one," the priest answered. "Now I must find men to bring Dwynwen back." He left them and strode down the street, calling, "Dwynwen of the Spring is dead. Who will help me bring her to the town?"

As he left with six men carrying a hurdle and white sheets to cover her on it, Joslin said, "I *will* find these things out. The priest may not ask, but we shall. If Meic is at sea, we shall ask Mared again."

They found Mared out in the fields, hoeing weeds from their plot. She straightened up, wiped her hands on her smock and listened as they asked their question. Her answer was the same as the priest's. "Dwynwen the anchoress was born the day she retreated from the world to the shrine. However much you want to know or need to know, I cannot sully Dwynwen's memory by telling you the person she was before she died by putting away sin and everything else in her old life. On that day she was born again. Someone else needs to tell you how she lived before, who has more right to do it than I do."

"Who is that person?" asked Joslin, very quietly. He was awed by Mared's sombre voice and severe expression.

"Someone you may never meet."

"Why not?"

"Long absence hides much. We didn't know Guillaume was dead."

"Has the answer to Joslin's question anything to do with Meic's voyage?" asked Gyll.

"Sometimes Meic goes to sea with his men and returns with an empty hold and we all starve," said Mared. "Sometimes he returns with a boat full of fish and we eat well and make money. One day, I fear he won't return at all. Who knows what this voyage will bring back?" She looked at Joslin's sad, doubt-ridden face. "You don't know what I'm talking about, do you?" she said. "But you will. I wish I could say more for your comfort now. But I fear I can't."

Meic's boat, with a brisk wind to sail into, a square sail to catch it and three strong men pushing on the steering tiller, was long out of sight of land. Nobody would consider going back until their task was finished, but with the morning a doubt had come and it still hung in the air. What they were doing was like shooting an arrow into the dark.

"There's no comfort in this place," said Joslin as they walked to the town. "They know more than they say. They're hiding something and conspiring not to tell me. And now there's a murderer among them, who chooses the moment we arrive to kill Dwynwen, our only hope."

"Joslin, do you really think anyone from this town would come creeping out in the night to kill Dwynwen of the Spring with his bare hands, when everybody here loved her?" said Gyll. "Think, Joslin, think."

"Who else but . . ." Joslin began – and stopped. He had a bad thought. "No. Not him. He went over the edge. He died at the waterfall."

"I didn't mean Lamb," said Gyll. "Think about Edmund Fitzgrace."

"Why Edmund?"

"Look," said Gyll. "Since we met again, two people have been murdered along our way. We left Rhys lying by the path because we thought they'd say we did it and hunt us down. But we weren't hunted. So who killed Rhys? I think that whoever killed Rhys killed Dwynwen and that person's very near now."

"Why Edmund?"

"It can't be James Lamb. He wasn't at Sycharth and now he's dead. And Edmund's involved in this. He thought Rhiannon was promised to him but she ran off with Guillaume. He would have been furious."

"Never," said Joslin. "People like him, they forget in a month while they batten on the next defenceless girl."

"You don't know that," Gyll replied. "He might have cared."

"Cared for what? He'd just want revenge for being thrown over in favour of a mere minstrel from France. That's what would really upset him.

Especially if he thought she'd had the minstrel's child."

"From what he said to Gruffydd that night, it seems he never married. He might have loved Rhiannon so much that nobody else was ever good enough," said Gyll.

"Not him," Joslin scoffed. "His sort aren't capable of it. If he didn't marry it was because no other family offered enough land and influence. To own Rhiannon, that's all he wanted."

"Back at Stovenham," said Gyll quietly, "Stephen de Noville loved his Lady Isobel, and she loved him. I mean *really* loved."

"All right," said Joslin. "Let's say Edmund murdered Rhys. Why?"

"Rhys helped Guillaume and Rhiannon escape from Sycharth. Then he helped us."

"Is that enough to kill a man?"

"It is if you think it's deepest treachery. It is if you're a spurned lover who thinks he's found the cause of his anger. It is if you feel your honour has been taken away."

"Honour?"

"Joslin, you know what knightly honour means to people like Edmund. It's the most important thing in their lives. He might have been a laughing stock for all these years. Dukes, earls, other knights, laughing behind his back and saying, 'Poor Edmund, bested by a Welsh girl and a French minstrel.' What's he going to do about it? "

"I don't know."

"Killing Rhys would be a start."

"Then why leave it so long? Why didn't he kill James Lamb?"

"Because nobody could ever nail James Lamb down to any one place. He came and went, with his own purposes and those of his masters, whoever they are. Edmund would love to see him dead. But James Lamb carried secrets and sometimes his sort are the ones you've got to keep alive, even though you hate them."

"Gyll, I don't understand you. First you say that Edmund loves Rhiannon, now you're saying he's going round killing everybody. Why would Edmund kill my mother?"

"Honour starts as something noble, but it can twist the person who holds it into doing evil. I've sat in the castle watching these knights and nobles from afar and seen it in them. I'm sure you have as well. If the anchoress was your mother, Edmund's sense of honour might tell him he must kill the one he loved, no matter what she was now. But what if she wasn't your mother? He must have recognized her and killed her for some other reason. What if the anchoress was Olwen? He might see her as being as guilty as Rhys."

Joslin didn't answer.

Then Gyll said, "All this time you've said that James Lamb killed Guillaume."

"He did," said Joslin. "I know he did."

"But what if he didn't? What if Edmund did? If Dwynwen was your mother and was once Rhiannon, then Edmund's revenge is complete at last. First, after years of searching, he found Guillaume and killed him. Then he found Rhiannon living as an anchoress and realized he could never have her, so he killed her as well. What more need he do?"

"If you're right, Edmund isn't going to leave me alive. While I live, I'm a reproach, a reminder, a danger to him. He has to wipe us all out. And if I go, then so do you."

They looked at each other for a moment as the full significance of this sank in. Then, as they entered Mared's house, Gyll said, "Then we're doomed together, you and I."

The *Newyddion Da* had anchored in a bay with a sandy beach and a high, green headland behind it. Meic had detailed two men to stay behind and guard the ship. The others landed and waded through the shallow sea to the shore. But they had not gone twenty paces before they heard hoofbeats and then a force of forty men on horseback, longhaired, rough-robed, well-armed, galloped round the headland. Some of Meic's men drew swords, but Meic said, "Put them away. We may be as good as dead already. If we threaten them, we surely are."

The leader gave high cries in a language Meic's men did not know, though some had heard it before. The horsemen slowed and surrounded them. Then the leader leant down from his horse and said, "You're not welcome here on Cormac's land. Be thankful we don't cut you down where you stand. You'll give up your weapons and come with us. Cormac will know what to do with you."

24

That evening, Mared came to them at the inn.

"Leave this place and stay with me while the men are away," she said. "My daughter is married and my son lost at sea, so it's lonely enough."

"No," said Joslin stubbornly. "Everyone knows what happened here but nobody tells us. You won't even tell the priest. I want help and I'm not getting any. I don't think we should stay in Aberffraw."

"Please come with me," Mared answered. "It's not that we won't help. We can't. Everyone wants, to but we didn't ask for what happened so many years ago and we don't know what happened in the end, so we can't answer your questions. But I'll say this: we have a secret which we can't reveal, not until Meic says, because it was his doing and it could go badly with him if the wrong people heard."

"What secret? You *must* tell me. *I'm* the one who should know," Joslin shouted.

"I can't," Mared said again. "But please come with me."

"Thank you," said Gyll. "Don't heed Joslin. We will."

Next day, Dwynwen of the Spring was buried in front of the altar where St Ursula's relic was now whole again. Joslin listened to the priest intoning prayers and wondered at the mystery of who she was and whose mother she had been. James Lamb's ominous words haunted his mind: *"You'll find proof . . ."* Also, after what Gyll had said, he felt an unsettling certainty that, somewhere round Aberffraw, someone hidden waited for them with murder in his heart. James Lamb's pockmarked sallow face and deformed mouth faded in Joslin's mind. The sharp, haughty features and short black beard remembered from one fleeting glimpse of Edmund Fitzgrace took their place. But it didn't matter who or what haunted him. He'd come all this way, given up his locket, found his mother – but he was hardly better off than when he left France. Everything shrieked out the same message: *What was it all for?*

One night he woke up and remembered that Dwynwen had told them how Rhiannon and Guillaume were married almost as soon as they came to Aberffraw. He listened to Gyll's quiet, easy breathing and wondered whether, the next morning, they should do the same. Then he thought – *no, not now. We should marry when we're happy and there's no shadow over us.* Then he wondered if there would ever be a time when there was no shadow over them.

Next day, Gyll joined Mared and worked with the women while Joslin went out in the fishing boats. Gyll and Mared went to the fishmarket to get the earliest catch and gutted the silver fish for the townsfolk and for people from round about who came to buy. Some of the fish were netted by Joslin, who learnt fast and thought he might enjoy life at sea. But then, why should he not? Winds were light, waters calm, nights cool and the sun bright and warm. A fisherman saw his contentment and said, "It's not always like this. You wait until the sea heaves, the wind blows and many good men don't come back."

That night, Joslin sang at the inn for the folk and life seemed good. But then the wind came, and rain and storm with it. All night, thunder rolled, lightning flashed and they prayed for Meic out at sea. Joslin could not sleep for the questions in his mind. What was James Lamb's proof? What was Meic's secret? Was the anchoress his mother? If she wasn't, *why had Guillaume lied to him about the key*? No answers came. Before dawn, he rose from his mattress and looked out. There was sudden bright, slow lightning and in it, looking straight at him, he saw the beard, glittering eyes and grim mouth of Edmund Fitzgrace.

"He was there, I tell you," Joslin insisted next morning. "We looked at each other. Then he nodded. I didn't like that nod. It was as if he was saying, 'I know where you are. I can come for you any time.' Then it was dark again. I didn't see where he went."

"Are you sure you didn't dream it?" asked Gyll.

"I *know* I didn't."

"Then stay in the cottage," said Gyll. "Don't go out in the boats."

"They won't let me go in this weather anyway," Joslin answered.

However, the rain and wind eased by morning and the storm blew itself out. Gyll said, "After the fishmarket I'll go into the fields with Mared. You stay inside and keep out of Edmund's way."

So Joslin stayed inside. But it was Gyll that Edmund Fitzgrace took.

Meic and his crew had survived and now they were leaving. But hardly had they put to sea than the storm came. They had a bad time of it. Often Meic thought their frail ship would break up in those huge seas. But, like all storms, it died away in the end, and now a fresh wind blew on Meic's face. He looked up at blue sky and fleecy clouds and said, "Sweet breeze, don't let us down, blow our precious cargo home."

"Joslin," Mared wailed "Gyll's disappeared. One moment she was hard at work and the next, she was gone. We were hoeing our plots and nobody kept an eye on her. Then someone asked, 'Where's Gyll?' and we saw she wasn't there. We looked round about, we called her in case she'd fallen and hurt herself, but there was no sign. It's as if the devil came and spirited her away."

"He has," Joslin answered. "I stayed indoors for protection, so it's Gyll he's taken. Mared, what shall we do?"

But Mared had no answer.

One moment Gyll was hoeing the patch Mared had given her, the next she was seized from behind, a strong hand clamped over her mouth, and she was bundled away. Her captor pushed her down so she was half crouching, then made her run, along rough tracks and past ragged clumps of trees. She struggled for breath. Then, far enough away for screams to be no use, she was hurled face-down on the ground. A knee was pressed on her back and a cloth knotted tightly round her eyes. Then, blindfold, she was pulled up again and shoved forward, made to run, only stopped from falling by a strong grasp on her shoulder. This breakneck, unseeing progress terrified her. Once, she found herself pushed through water nearly up to her waist. She was ready to drop when she heard the roar of the sea. Only now did her captor let her stand upright. She was pushed forward again and now was ploughing through something sodden which held her feet back. She guessed it was wet sand. Soon the sand turned dry and sharp marram grass stung her legs – they were on sand dunes, climbing in cloying sand which made her legs heavy like lead,. She guesses she must have reached the top of this summit – and then there was another violent push from behind. Then they were descending and she feared to fall forward and have her face buried. But at last the dunes were over, and now the ground was hard and wet underfoot. She heard faint rustling. Water sometimes dripped on her face. There was a smell of long-rotted leaves. At last they slowed and she was let go.

She sank to the ground exhausted, and great retching breaths rasped up from deep inside her. The blindfold was torn off. There was a roof over her head and walls round her. Water still dripped on her. She was in a tiny, dark shelter. Two walls were merely old planks propped up against solid stone. In one of the wooden walls was an entrance draped with sacking. Draughts knifed through gaps in the planking and the stone walls exuded cold. When she had her breath back, she looked up and at last saw the face of her captor. Though she had only seen it for an instant back at Sycharth she knew it at once. Edmund.

A cold shudder ran through her body as she thought of Dwynwen strangled on her mattress. She swallowed and said nothing.

Edmund spoke. "Where is your minstrel?"

"I don't know," she replied.

"Yes, you do," said Edmund. "He was in Aberffraw last night and I doubt whether he's moved too far away since."

Gyll did not answer. Edmund said, "If he's fishing, I shall wait for him. If he's in the cottage, I shall rouse him out. I want you both here."

Now Gyll spoke, hotly, full of anger. "What for? So you can kill us, like you killed his mother? Like you probably killed Guillaume in France? Like you killed Rhys?"

Even in the half-light, she saw his expression alter. What surprised her was that it did not change to fury, but deep, deep sadness.

"My dear girl," he said. "There is so very much that you don't know."

First, Joslin and the women searched close to the strips of land that the folk worked. Then they ranged in circles round the fields as far as the sands. Nothing. They crept back wearily to the town. Joslin threw himself on his bed at Mared's and groaned with this new loss.

Mared stood over him. "Joslin," she said. "Think. You must think. You know her better than we do. What is she likely to do?"

"She'll remain steadfast and faithful, even though she dies for it," he replied. Then he thought of her with Edmund Fitzgrace. "With a man like that, die she surely will."

There was a sudden commotion in the street. Voices shouted in joy. Joslin sat up, hope on his face. "They've found her," he cried.

No. It was a different cry – "Meic is near. Our men are returning. The *Newyddion Da* is just off Carreg-y-trai."

Gyll was scornful. "I know everything," she said. "I know how Guillaume took Rhiannon from you. I know how James Lamb used everybody, Guillaume, Rhiannon, Olwen, Rhys, and now you as well, in his scheming. I know how Rhiannon and Guillaume came to Aberffraw and James Lamb lost their track because of the ferryman. I know that Olwen followed and she and Rhiannon were both pregnant. I know you were angry that a low French minstrel had bested you."

"Any more?" said Edmund.

"No. Dwynwen the anchoress was murdered before she could tell us the rest. You murdered her."

"What reason would I have for doing that?"

"You didn't want us to hear any more of her story."

"Not so," said Edmund. "To prove it, I'll tell it now, to the finish."

"You'll tell me lies," said Gyll.

"A true knight does not lie," Edmund answered. "And I am a true knight. Now, let's see what you know Start with who Joslin's father is."

"I think Guillaume is Joslin's father and Rhiannon is his mother," said Gyll.

"You mean you hope they are. Olwen had James Lamb's child. Do you know where Olwen's child is?"

"No," said Gyll.

"I don't think you known very much at all. If you did, you'd never think me capable of such a dreadful crime as killing Joslin's mother. And I would certainly never kill Rhys, a good servant to a master I respect. What do you mean by saying I killed Joslin's mother?"

"Dwynwen. The anchoress. You strangled her."

"But you said Rhiannon was Joslin's mother."

"I said I *think* she was. I might be wrong."

"But anchoresses are all holy women. I wouldn't dare kill her. Why should I kill Rhys?"

"To stop him telling us what happened all those years ago?"

"A drastic way of shutting his mouth. Why ever should you think I killed Guillaume?"

"Because you were with the English lords in France. You'd searched for Guillaume and found him at last, in the count's castle. You wanted revenge for how he'd made you look a fool and for how he'd brought a message from Owain Lawgoch which could make more wars between Wales and England. So you killed him."

"All those murders," said Edmund. "I'm a terrible man, aren't I? You think I'd kill for any reason and none. Well, I don't deny I could have killed Guillaume all those years ago at Sycharth, and I don't deny I was with the English embassage to the Count of Treauville's castle in France. We had urgent business, and yes, it was to do with Wales and what to do about Owain Lawgoch. He'd become a nuisance to both sides. His greed and his underhand actions were stopping us from fighting a true chivalrous war between noble knights. Both French and English wanted an end of him. But remember, James Lamb was there as well. Didn't he also have cause to kill Guillaume?"

"Joslin thinks so. But James didn't kill Rhys, because he wasn't at Sycharth, and he didn't strangle the anchoress – because he's dead."

Gyll could see that this gave Edmund a shock. "Dead?" he said. "James Lamb dead? What do you mean, *dead*?"

Gyll told him about Joslin's encounter at the standing stones and the waterfall. Edmund listened, then said, "If James *is* dead, and as I am innocent, you have a deep and serious job finding the murderer. I would not like to be in your shoes."

"But it's you," Gyll insisted. "It has to be."

"Nothing *has* to be," Edmund answered. "Nothing is ever what it seems. You'll find that's true when you see how all Joslin's hopes are dashed in front of him."

"I don't believe you," said Gyll.

"Then listen," Edmund replied.

25

Joslin's mind was whirling. Gyll's disappearance was tearing him apart. He had to keep looking. They had been discouraged too easily before, nobody had stopped to think, and now the townsfolk had forgotten Gyll and gone running off to the harbour because Meic was coming back.

First, he should go back to the fields and search where she was last seen. He left Mared's cottage and soon stood where Gyll had disappeared. If nobody saw her go, they must have been hoeing with their backs to her. Edmund, if it *was* Edmund, must have hidden nearby. To get her away unseen, he must have taken her eastwards, towards Newborough. Only on that side were there rocks and bushes as cover. Otherwise he would have been in full view of the working men. He looked for traces of a capture. Nothing.

He could see the sand dunes towards Newborough. If they'd gone through them, he reasoned, there would be footprints. If they hadn't he'd be further away from finding Gyll than ever. But he had to try this way.

He ran from the fields across the hummocky, stony land towards Malltraeth Sand, waded across Afon Cefni and skirted the coast until he reached where the dry dunes stretched away before him. Here he stopped. In the sands were footprints, two sets, one large, one small.

He breathed a prayer of thanks. Then he followed the tracks up and down the sloping sides of the dunes until he saw trees ahead, grown as an attempt to hold the sand back. He lost the trail, but carried on through the trees, reasoning that Edmund would have done the same. Once through the trees he saw Newborough ahead.

But what was this? Half-covered by sand, and ruined by war, was a crumbling stone wall. He walked round it and found a once imposing entrance. Now, gateposts stood with no gates. Within the walls were the remains of a large timber-framed hall and other smaller buildings made of stone. All roofless now, desolate, deserted.

He knew where he must be. Rhosyr, the palace of the princes of Gwynedd – until the English had put paid to it. Of course – Edmund might well hide here, because his father was one of the English soldiers who ruined it.

But where in the ruins might Edmund hide? Joslin paused at the entrance, looked and listened. In the far corner was a smaller shelter: planks formed rough walls against the stone, with a roof made of turves over more planks with their ends projecting untidily. Sacking had been nailed over the nearest wall, to cover a way in. Cautiously he crept towards it.

He heard voices. The man's voice might be Edmund's. But the girl's was, without any doubt, Gyll's, and he had to gulp down a cry of delight which would give his presence away. Instead, he made himself very small against the wall, and listened.

Edmund seemed in no hurry. When he spoke, his voice was gentle and his face had softened. "Your name, I believe, is Gyll," he said. She nodded. "Well, Gyll, I mean you no harm. And I mean your Joslin no harm either. Please believe me."

He studied her unmoving face, as if hoping for a response.

"You're right," he continued. "When I found that Guillaume had spoken to Rhiannon I was very angry. How dare he? A minstrel, hardly better than a servant, and French at that, presuming to say words of love to a lady higher above him in birth than the eye can measure? What betrayal of God's ordained scheme of things was this? Yes, I would have killed him like a dog. I said as much to Gruffydd. And more – Rhiannon was promised to me, she was a Welsh girl betrothed to a member of one of the foremost families in the English realm. No girl from a conquered race could ask for greater fortune. Yet she spurned it. That night, when she and the minstrel fled, my anger was all-consuming. For a while."

"What do you mean, for a while?" said Gyll.

He answered in a gentle, almost longing voice. "When James brought the Lady Isobel de Noville from Newtown to Dolforwyn Castle where I was staying, she told me about the ambush in the forest and that she had absolved you from your duty, because you kept your love for another French minstrel close in your heart and God allowed you to find him again by a miracle. The story she told touched my heart. You see, Gyll, even a knight has a heart to touch. That is why I can speak thus to you, though you too are a mere servant and I am a nobleman. *You* will understand – though you may not believe it – that when I found Rhiannon was gone my anger strangely died. I realized something which my pride had concealed from me. I thought I had wanted Rhiannon as a convenience, a beautiful possession, as well as a means to an end, to unite the fortunes of the foremost English and Welsh families along the Marches. But when she was gone, I found my loss was not just at losing a precious object. I realized, Gyll, that I truly loved her. This surprised me. I had never thought myself capable of love. Do you believe me?"

Gyll repeated what she had said to Joslin. "Stephen de Noville loved the Lady Isobel," she said. "Yes, I do believe you."

"Thank you for that," he said. "But I was still angry with James because he had tricked me as he had tricked Gruffydd and Rhys, and now he was gone as well. But we didn't set out to hunt anyone down. Gruffydd was distraught because he loved Rhiannon as a daughter and she had spurned him. He would have had the dogs set after them both. I wouldn't let him. I wished them no harm. Neither of us dared hunt James Lamb."

"Why not?" asked Gyll.

"Because he's a confidential spy for King Edward himself. He carries more secrets in his head than any man alive, about the king's friends as well as his enemies. He's important to many high people in this land, and he knows things to their discredit – but no one dare harm him because if they do they'll have the king and his chancellor to answer to."

Gyll let that information sink in silently.

"And I knew why he was at Sycharth. I knew he'd been in France, that he'd convinced Owain Lawgoch to take him on as his advisor and was there when Owain gave Guillaume that call to arms for the Welsh. I knew he'd smoothed Guillaume's entry into England, and then left Owain on some pretext so he could slip through England and go to Sycharth. He knew Guillaume would be there sooner or later. He thought that Gruffydd would reject Owain's call, arrest Guillaume and give Owain's letter to King Edward as another reason to make war on France. What rewards Gruffydd would then receive. And James as well.'

"But it didn't work out. Gruffydd gave the letter back to Guillaume and let him go on his way. James had no Guillaume, no letter and no chance to do anything about it while he was a guest in Gruffydd's house. That's why he went in chase of them when they escaped. H*e had* to have that letter."

"Olwen followed them," said Gyll.

"Yes," said Edmund. "Yes, she did."

Joslin heard those last words. Amazed by Edmund's friendliness, he had worked himself closer to the shelter until he almost leant on it, with his ear to a gap in the boarding. As he shifted to make himself comfortable he brushed against a board and it slipped lightly. He froze at once.

"What was that?" said Edmund sharply.

"I heard nothing," Gyll answered.

Edmund listened. Then he said, "No one can know we're here." He recollected his thoughts. "It was some months before we saw James again," he continued. "He returned to Sycharth and sent word to me at Chirk to join him there. He had been sent on a wild goose chase to Ireland. So he'd taken ship there and searched the English earldoms and the lands of Irish chieftains, until he realized he'd been tricked himself. He was toweringly angry. But he had found out a lot. He knew now where they went."

"Aberffraw," said Gyll.

"Yes. But they had moved on again. James didn't know where. The people of Aberffraw feigned ignorance. And things were not as they used to be. Olwen had been with them in Aberffraw. Both women were with child, Rhiannon by Guillaume and Olwen -"

"By James Lamb," Gyll interrupted.

"Yes. But here comes the thing which will ruin Joslin's world. One child was dead. The mother had miscarried."

"Which one?" said Gyll, pale with sudden misgiving.

"Rhiannon. Joslin is the son of James Lamb and Olwen. James Lamb himself told me."

"Who could believe a word James Lamb says?"

"But James was not making this up. No. The chief man of Aberffraw – what is his name? - Meic, he it was who told him. You can't doubt his word, surely."

Joslin heard. For a second he sat like a block of ice, his heart beating so slowly that he thought it would stop. "*You'll find pro . . .*" James Lamb had said – and this was it. No wonder the people of Aberffraw would tell him nothing. Then he sprang back into life. He hurled himself round the wooden wall to the entrance, tore the sacking away and burst into the shelter. He saw Edmund's hateful, haughty noble's face and Gyll's grey eyes even wider than usual with surprise. He threw himself on Edmund, butted him against the stone wall and shouted, "*You lie, you lie. You and Lamb together. It's not true.*

Edmund pushed him back against Gyll as if flicking away a fly. "But it is true, Joslin. I'm deeply sorry, but it is. You never know who your real friends are, do you? Everything that has ever happened to you sprang from what your Meic told James Lamb all those years ago. Once Lamb heard that, he wanted his own son back, and he has sought you ever since."

"So that's Mared's secret," said Gyll. "She, Meic and the others were conspiring not to tell us."

"James Lamb is not my father," Joslin cried. "I'll never believe it."

"But the anchoress," Gyll asked Edmund. "Surely she was Rhiannon?"

"I know nothing about the anchoress. How could she be Rhiannon? You said her name was Dwynwen. How can anchoresses be promised to

English knights, run away with minstrels and bear their children?"

Joslin sat up, broke away from Gyll and looked angrily at Edmund. "You lie again," he said. "Lamb's dead. Only you could have murdered Dwynwen, to pay her back for what she did to you. You murdered Rhys as well – you were there, and Lamb wasn't. You might have murdered my father as well."

Edmund looked gravely at him. "Joslin," he said. "I have killed many people in my time, in battle, single combat and as a matter of honour. But I swear to you, as a true knight, that I never killed Rhys or Dwynwen or Guillaume, if you still insist on saying he's your father."

"Were you in Joslin's castle when Guillaume was killed?" said Gyll.

"Yes," said Edmund. "I know Guillaume was stabbed and you, Joslin, fled. But I didn't see Guillaume killed."

"Have you no idea, no suspicions?" asked Gyll. "Could it have been James?"

Edmund said nothing.

"That means it was," said Joslin. "So I've had my revenge already, now his body is at the bottom of a waterfall."

"Will you ever be told?" said Edmund. "You haven't revenged your father. You've killed him. Or you think you have."

Joslin looked him straight at him. "I'll never believe that," he said.

"I know you won't until you see once and for all that you have to, when you hear it from Meic's own mouth," said Edmund. "And I won't believe James Lamb is dead until I see his body inside a coffin, the lid hammered down with the biggest nails ever made, then the whole thing buried fifteen feet deep and covered with boulders the size of sarsen stones, so he can never rise again."

"James Lamb is dead," Joslin repeated. "He fell over the edge. I know he did."

"Listen," said Gyll suddenly.

"What is it?" said Edmund.

"I heard something outside."

They emerged from the shelter and looked round.

"Nothing," said Edmund.

"You imagined it," said Joslin.

But Gyll was sure she had seen a shape, no more than a shadow, flit through where the gates used to be and then disappear.

26

"We should stop this," said Edmund. "We've found each other, you know I'm not to be feared, at least by you, and we'll go to Aberffraw together. The people there will tell you that what I say is true. Think what you like of me, but for now we should call a truce and work together."

"It was James Lamb who told you about Rhiannon's baby dying," said Joslin. "He could still be lying. Perhaps Meic never said such a thing." He wasn't going to give up hope.

"Lamb doesn't always lie" Edmund answered.

"He said I should stay clear of you. He said that beside you, he was so meek that he really was a lamb. Was that a lie as well?"

"I'm a fierce enemy and I know my rights and my place," said Edmund. "But to you I choose to be a friend."

"He said my mother loved him and rejected Guillaume and you."

"Strangely, Joslin, that may be true. Olwen did love him, and it seems she was your mother."

"*No!*" Joslin shouted.

Edmund went on. "Rhiannon would have laughed in Lamb's face."

They came out of the trees and crossed the dunes. When they were through them, Edmund said, "You have not asked why I, a knight, abase myself by skulking round like a common beggar."

"I don't need to," said Joslin. "You called me spy and traitor at Sycharth. Lamb warned me against you. I knew you'd come after us."

"That's not the reason. It happened when I was at Dolforwyn castle by Abermule. One night, James Lamb, who I hadn't seen for all those years, came to the castle escorting the Lady Isobel de Noville. I heard the story of your marvellous meeting, and then I knew I had to see you, Joslin, to put all straight between us, because those events have weighed heavily on me. I have never married, and never wanted to, since Rhiannon left me. Lamb said he would guide me to you. We followed your trail through Wales as far as some God-forsaken settlement miles from anywhere, and then I said, 'Surely he will go to Sycharth.' James was sure you wouldn't, but I knew I had to see for myself. I came alone to Sycharth to find you there already, singing like Guillaume. I tried to have you brought to me as a spy and traitor but Gruffydd would have none of it. 'Then I'll see you tomorrow,' I said to myself, never thinking that history would repeat itself, you'd escape in the night and Rhys would help you. And then Rhys was murdered."

"You did it," said Joslin.

"That's not true. I liked Rhys. He was a fine steward to his master. I believe Lamb came to Sycharth and hid. I believe Rhys found him. James wormed out of Rhys that he was helping you escape. Then he killed him. He knew you'd be blamed for this murder."

"Why weren't we hunted?" said Joslin.

"Because I stopped it. I told Gruffydd what I thought had happened and he agreed to let me deal with James Lamb in my own way. Because deal with him I will, Joslin. Once and for all."

"Joslin, you must trust Edmund," said Gyll.

"Why should I?" Joslin asked.

"He has his honour. To him, people like us aren't worth lying to."

The *Newyddion Da* was off the island, Carreg-y-trai, becalmed as the winds died. Little boys ran from the harbour along the rocks to the headland of Braich Lwyd, cheering, shouting and urging the ship along. By late afternoon, the winds freshened again. Soon the ship was in the shelter of Braich Lwyd and entering Afon Ffraw. Then it was poled up the river's narrow channel between shore and sand to its mooring place, as the sail was hauled down. The voyage was over.

As they walked, Joslin's mind was full of strange feelings. He'd never believe his parents were James Lamb and Olwen. Lamb must have lied as he lied about everything. Including the story that Meic told him – that it was Rhiannon's child who died. Yet Mared *had* said there was a secret . . .

No, he couldn't work it out. Best to keep to what he was quite sure of. *James Lamb was dead.* He refused to believe he had killed his own father. He had no father – and now, with the murder of Dwynwen, no mother either.

Joslin looked at Edmund through narrowed eyes. If Dwynwen was Rhiannon in her former life, Edmund would surely never have killed her. But if she was Olwen – well, he might. But why?

Edmund walked quickly, saying nothing, as if turning something important over in his mind. "I must tell you this – even though telling such as you should be unthinkable," he said. "If I saw Rhiannon after all these years, now we are older and wiser, I would say, 'Rhiannon, marry me, and let us forget those terrible days nineteen years ago.'"

"You can only say that now Guillaume's dead," said Joslin. And then he opened his eyes wide again as a great light dawned, and he cried, "Of course. You *did* kill him."

"No," Edmund said. "Never. Never in this world."

The *Newyddion Da* tied up at the quayside. Mared and the women stood at the edge waiting. The crew climbed out one by one. Each married man sought out his wife and children, but did not lead them off to their homes. They stood and faced the ship. There was a strange air of expectancy.

Mared waited patiently for Meic who, as ship's master, was last to leave. And so did everybody else.

The town was deserted. No rope was being made, no produce sold. Dogs wandered, pigs rooted, cats slept.

They came to the harbour. Gyll and Joslin hung back, because the return of the *Newyddion Da* was the town's business, not theirs. But they were seen and, to their surprise, they were handed through until they stood on the quayside next to Mared, as Meic prepared to leave the ship. But he was not alone. A veiled figure stood by him and Joslin saw that it was a woman. Meic helped her up and willing hands brought her out until she stood on firm ground.

Meic saw Joslin. "Joslin," he called. "We went on this voyage in the hope that you might know the truth about yourself at last. The ship was well named. *Newyddion Da* is, in English, *Good News.* And I believe we have brought an answer which you'll agree really is good news."

The woman took her veil off.

A sigh came from everyone there. Here was a beautiful lady with deep brown eyes, though her dark hair showed flecks of grey. A strange leap of the heart cut short any sound Joslin might have made.

The lady looked round. She saw the welcoming folk of Aberffraw. She saw Joslin and Gyll. Then she looked at who stood behind them and the smile disappeared.

"Edmund?" she said.

"Rhiannon," said Edmund.

Rhiannon's smile died on her face. Joslin's limbs seemed frozen.

Edmund knelt at Rhiannon's feet. "My lady," he said, "many years ago I offered you my hand, and a bargain was made between our families. Then you broke our betrothal for the Frenchman, and for all these years I have known nothing of you. Now, so strangely, we meet again, and the Frenchman is dead. I have no malice in my heart, only a love which has grown through years of separation. I ask you to think afresh, look on me with favour and say we are betrothed anew."

Rhiannon spoke. Her voice was clear and gentle and Joslin thought of his recent dreams. "Edmund," she said. "I would not marry you then and I will not marry you now even if I were free to."

"I'm sorry," said Edmund. "I have surprised you. This is too sudden, too unexpected. Think on what I have said, I beg you."

"Yes, Edmund, I will think on it because I would never treat your words with contempt. But I will not change my mind."

There was sudden steel in Edmund's voice. "You will, my lady," he said. He turned to Joslin. All his friendliness was gone. His expression was vindictive, contemptuous. "It is an affront to God Himself that a churl like you should ever think this lady is your mother," he snarled. "You're the son of a maidservant, and a devious wretch who thought nothing of her. Rhiannon's child was miscarried. Nothing alters that. Meic here said so."

There was a silence so profound that a sudden surge of water against the quay startled everyone. Joslin struggled with conflicting thoughts: *I wish this woman was my mother and Guillaume's wife. But if she is, then my father lied to me as he died – for why else did the anchoress have the key?* Then: *Lamb's lies are worse. He lied to Edmund about Meic. I won't believe it.* He cried, "It's not true. Tell him, Meic."

"I'm sorry, Joslin," Meic replied. "It is. That's what we said. I can't deny it. We had good reason."

Gyll thought she had seen a shadow flit through the gates of Rhosyr and she was right. The man hid outside, waiting until the three had passed, then followed unobserved, something he had done so well for so many years. He stayed within earshot and heard everything that was said. Not even Joslin's honed instinct alerted him to the danger. But how could Joslin think he was followed by one he knew to be dead? The notion amused the man. *I am a returner from the grave,* he thought.

When they reached the harbour he took a vantage point on a wall where he could see and hear everything. The lady took her veil off and he saw she was Rhiannon. Then Edmund knelt and made his speech, and it was all he could do not to laugh out loud.

He heard Edmund repeat what Meic had told him years before and on which he had based so much of his life – that Rhiannon's child was miscarried. Then Meic said, "We had good reason."

Of course the man had good reason to say it – it was true. Then doubt bored a hole in his brain. Was Meic saying he'd had good reason to lie? Had these churls, these low-born Welsh creatures, lied to *him,* James Lamb, who lived his life by lying to others? And had he actually *believed* them? The more he thought about it, the more sure he was that it must so. He'd already found the anchoress and recognized her. She had told him something which amounted to the same lie. Though he didn't believe her, he had killed her to stop her repeating it to Joslin. But he didn't like that "*We had good reason.*" If these Welshmen lied to him and he, who cheated others, had been cheated, then how could he ever trust his instincts again?

What would Rhiannon say now? Edmund must never know what it was. It was time to act.

It was as if a dark angel, or the devil himself, or the huge black spider of Joslin's dreams, descended on them with dreadful suddenness and then vanished. But in that instance, one sinuous arm hooked round Edmund's throat and the other plunged a knife deep in his back. The body pitched forward with a gurgling cry and the death-dealer was gone before anyone could draw breath.

After the first moment's shock, Joslin knew he had just seen how, with strong arm and smooth stab, his father and Rhys had died. At last he knew he had been right all along about who killed Guillaume. And yet . . .

"That was James Lamb," he stammered. "But he's dead."

A few men ran off after the killer, but they soon came back shaking their heads. "Let him go," said Meic. "I won't put our own folk in danger on his account."

Gill took Joslin's arm and led him forward. "Forget him," she said. "This is the woman

Guillaume married. She is your mother. Speak to her at last."

But Rhiannon was crouching over Edmund's body. "Edmund," she sobbed. "I did you great wrong once and it has led you to a terrible death. I am sorry."

She cradled his head in her arms and kissed his forehead. Joslin stood by at a loss. So many times he had pictured this meeting, but never thought of anything like this.

Meic spoke. "This death is bad for us," he said. "An English knight has been murdered and Aberffraw will be blamed."

"No," said the priest. "I was witness and I will be believed. We must take him to Beaumaris and give him over to the English for he is own of their own. We know who did it and if I know anything, so will they. They'll send a coroner out here, but we needn't fear him."

Rhiannon looked up. "I shall go with Edmund," she said.

"That you won't," said Meic. "If the English see you they'll take you and Gruffydd Fychan will shut you away or put you in a nunnery. And where will your son be then?"

"My son?" she said, bewildered. Then she saw who stood beside her. Her face suddeny broke into a glorious smile. She rose from Edmund's body and embraced him. "Joslin, my son, Joslin," she cried. And then, fearfully, "Where is Guillaume?"

Edmund's body lay in the church. Next day, the priest and a party of men would take him to

Beaumaris. James Lamb had disappeared into thin air. "We've seen the last of him," said Meic. Yet Joslin was uneasy.

Rhiannon stayed with Joslin and Gyll in Meic's house. At last, Joslin could tell Rhiannon his story, of Guillaume's murder and his own year-long quest.

"I knew Guillaume must be dead when I saw you here alone," said Rhiannon and lowered her head so nobody could see her face.

"I'm not alone," Joslin replied. "I have Gyll." Then he asked Meic the question which bothered him so much. "Why did you tell James Lamb that Rhiannon's child had been miscarried?"

"To keep him away from here," Meic replied. "I also told him that Guillaume, Rhiannon and Olwen had gone far away and we didn't know where. It was not true, yet he believed it and left us alone. I think he wanted to believe it."

"He in turn told Edmund, who believed it as well," said Joslin. "Edmund told me. But why did you keep it from me when we came here? Didn't you trust me when I said who I was?"

"Joslin, everyone who was alive then knew who you were at once. But nobody would tell you the truth. I had told a lie which weighed heavily on me for years. I was the only one would could explain it, and I wouldn't do that until I knew we could face you properly and tell you the whole truth. We remembered how Lamb followed Rhiannon and Guillaume. Someone might be following you as well, someone who might hear, seize you and force the truth out of you. And we were right, weren't we?

227

Besides, we didn't know where Rhiannon was. We knew where we had left her, but we had no idea what happened to her afterwards."

"Where did you leave her?" asked Gyll.

"All in good time," said Meic. "Here is the truth. It was Olwen's and Lamb's child that was miscarried. We knew where Olwen was and we knew something of where Rhiannon and Guillaume might be. But we'd tell Lamb none of this, for fear that knowing his child was dead would drive him to a frenzy and then he would consider what we said a little more deeply."

"What do you mean?" Joslin asked.

"Guillaume and Rhiannon were indeed far across the sea. We had taken them there ourselves. But Olwen was very near."

"Ah, I see," said Gyll. "So the anchoress was Olwen. She thought her miscarriage was God punishing her sin, so she wiped out her old life, and turned to God and the shrine as a penance. She became Dwynwen."

"She did," said Meic. "We reckoned that if Lamb knew she'd miscarried, and then heard about the anchoress at the shrine, he'd work it out for himself. He had to be kept from her."

"But I think he found her in the end," said Gyll.

"What do you mean?" Rhiannon asked. So they told her and Rhiannon said, "She was my friend as well as my servant. I shall grieve for her. We will go to the shrine tomorrow."

"I think that when we first went there, James Lamb followed us. As Olwen was telling us the story, he was very close, listening," said Gyll. "Then he realized who she was. He heard her say she could tell us no more, because some memories were so bitter that she could never be free of them. She couldn't speak them and we mustn't ask her to. He must have wondered what she meant. Maybe he suspected then that Meic might not have told him the truth after all. What might the anchoress tell us next day? He didn't know, but if it was to tell us that her most bitter memory was of her own baby dying, he had to kill her to stop her mouth. Perhaps he made her say it to him before he strangled her."

"But that would mean my own eyes deceived me at the waterfall," said Joslin. "Lamb's not dead, after all, and he's been following us since I came down the mountain alone." He turned to Meic. "Where did you find my mother?" he asked.

"Where we left her and lost her. In Ireland."

"Why Ireland?" said Joslin.

"Ah, Joslin," said Mared. "So many secrets. And now you know them all except the last, and only Rhiannon can tell us that."

"It's late," said Rhiannon. "My voyage has been long and hard, and too many things, both sad and joyous, have happened today. Tomorrow, Joslin and Gyll, we'll go to the shrine and there I'll finish the story Olwen started. Now, I must sleep."

27

The rain had cleared. The morning was fine, breezy and brisk. As they passed the rock and came to the bubbling spring, the cave with the altar and Dwynwen's cell, the crows were gone and birds sang again. Rhiannon stood outside the cave. "How fresh the air is," she said. "Whether you knew her as Olwen or Dwynwen, her spirit is here."

She went into the cell. Her face was grave. "She never forgot why she was here, and she never forgot Guillaume and me," she said. "Why else take the name of Dwynwen? It's a strange name for an anchoress."

"Why?" asked Gyll.

"Dwynwen is the Welsh patron saint of lovers. She has her own shrine at Llandwyn. She wanted all loves either to be together or cured of their love. For Olwen, the wish was granted. Guillaume and I were together, Olwen was cured of her love. Or if she was not, she never let me know."

"Finish the story," said Joslin. "The last thing Olwen told us was that you were both with child."

"Yes," said Rhiannon. "I was so happy, but Olwen was sad because she loved the child's father once, and he had played her false. Yet we both found pleasure in feeling our children grow, knowing we were bringing new life into the world. Guillaume was attentive to us both: he was always kind to Olwen. But all was not well with her. I shall never forget the night she miscarried. She would have no baby after all. She lay on the very edge of life, praying for the death she said she deserved for her sin. But death never came. When she was well again she said, 'God has spared me for a purpose. He will tell me what it is in His own good time.'"

"Only then did Guillaume show her the relic of St Ursula that he carried. 'The saint has protected me through my trouble,' Olwen cried. 'If she's here, no harm can come. I shall serve God all my life through her.'

"Then news came from Holyhead. A man with a sallow face had landed from Ireland, angry after months of vain searching, claiming that a ferryman had tricked him and vowing to find a fugitive couple that he knew were on the island. He would pay well for information about a Welsh lady and a French minstrel.

"Some drunken fool blabbed out that he knew of two pregnant women who shouldn't be here. The others shut him up, and willing folk came down from Holyhead to warn us – this man would come to Aberffraw sooner or later. 'If he's come from Ireland,' said Meic, 'then, it looks as if Ireland may be the best place to take you to keep out of his way. Make ready for the journey.' With heavy heart, Guillaume and I did so. But Olwen said no. She was

Welsh and would not leave. She would make a
shrine to St Ursula and watch over it all her life.
Then she cried, 'But I can't take the saint's
protection away from you.' 'The relic is a joined
knucklebone,' said Guillaume. 'If we take it apart at
the join we break nothing. We will all have Ursula's
protection. Keep your half for the shrine. One day,
someone will come to fit the whole together:
Rhiannon, me, or –' 'Or a girl called Gwynedd,
Welsh after the line of princes,' I said. 'Or a boy
called Joslin, in the French style,' said Guillaume."

Joslin let out a long sigh. "She remembered,"
he said. Then he recalled what had kept him awake
these past nights. "Guillaume said there was only one
key to the locket, and it belonged to you. That's why
I thought the anchoress must be my mother. Why
did she have the key? I've been tortured for days
now thinking my father's last words to me were a
lie."

Rhiannon laughed. Then she saw the pain on
Joslin's face and stopped. "I'm sorry, Joslin.
Guillaume would never, never have willingly misled
you. I knew him so well. Tell me exactly what he
said."

"I'll never forget," Joslin replied. "'*There is
only one key...and it belongs to your mother. Find
her . . . and know why all this has been.*' Then he
died." As he spoke he saw again his father's dying
face, blood soaking the deck and the minstrel's tunic
he still wore from that last feast in the castle.

"So you thought that whoever gave you the key
would be your mother?" said Rhiannon.

"Yes," answered Joslin.

"But it needn't be so. He said, '*belongs*'. The key does belong to me and always will. But Olwen held it in trust for me, because we asked her to. Something held in trust does not belong to the person who holds it. The locket and key are mine. My father gave them to me, with a curl of my mother's hair inside. I took the curl out, put the relic in, locked it and gave Olwen the key."

"Why didn't Guillaume tell me?" said Joslin.

"But don't you see? He would have. Guillaume was a minstrel, a storyteller. It was his life. Like yours. *'Find her and know why this has been.'* It almost sounds like the beginning of a ballad, as if he had said, '*Now hear the tale of all that did befall,*' just as you might say before you sing one of your songs. Even as he died, Guillaume couldn't help starting to tell you a story. I think he would have told you to hear the rest from Olwen, and then find Meic and his ship to bring you to me. Poor Guillaume: he died even before he could start."

His mother was right – Joslin knew it now and felt almost ashamed at not thinking of it for himself. Then he realized that if his father had stayed alive for just a few more minutes his journey might have been very different. For one thing, he would never have met Gyll.

Rhiannon continued. "Meic had made the ship ready and got his crew together for us. Before we left, we all had to agree on what Meic would tell Lamb. We knew this would be difficult, because how can you fool such a cunning man? We thought long and hard."

"Has anybody fooled James Lamb for long?" Joslin said.

"Here is what we decided to say," said Rhiannon. "The three of us had stolen out of the town one night: Meic and his people had no idea where. Olwen and I had been pregnant but one child had been miscarried. But which one would they tell him? At first, we thought they should tell the truth, because if Lamb thought his child was dead and we'd all disappeared he might lose interest in us. Then we thought we should lie because he might think a lady's son worth searching for, a servant's not at all. Then Mared said that knowing his own child was alive might drive him mad, and he'd be more likely to search for it.

"Now we were in a real quandary. Who knew how he would react? In the end, we thought we must tell him my child miscarried and his lived, but keep secret that Olwen was staying here at the shrine. It seemed the best thing to do. If he found my child and took it back to Sycharth, he would be well rewarded by Gruffydd. Nobody would want a servant's baby. But we thought he might want to search for his own child, and we didn't want him anywhere near Olwen. So we were very unhappy – whatever we said, there would be great risks." She looked at the ground before she spoke again. "I'm very sorry, Joslin. I think we chose wrong."

"How could you tell what Lamb would do?" said Joslin. "He thought that Guillaume would treat Olwen's child as his own, and this angered him. He wanted me for himself. He wanted his son back. That's why he searched for so long."

"We sailed at night," Rhiannon continued. "The afternoon before, Guillaume, Olwen and I walked out here to the spring. 'The shrine will be here,' Olwen said. 'The bishop will bless it and I shall be its anchoress. I ask no more.' That night we left, in great sadness. The voyage was rough: we feared for our lives. When we dropped anchor off Howth, near Dublin, it was like the end of a long, bad dream. Meic left men to guard the ship and picked an armed band to go ashore, for he vowed to see us safe before he came away again.

"But he never did. We were stopped at once by fierce, armed Irishmen and we thought our lives were finished. But they treated us well. They took us to Cormac, their chieftain. Cormac allowed Meic no further. 'This is our land and we decide what happens to those who come to its shores,' he said. Then he said, 'Are these the two that that devil from England, a man I'd trust no further than a dog can spit, was looking for?' 'They are,' said Meic. 'Then give them over to me,' said Cormac. So we had to leave Meic and saw him and his crew no more. 'Don't fear us,' said Cormac. 'I know where to take you for proper protection.' After four shivering days we came to a castle. Cormac shouted out for entry and the drawbridge was let down. Guillaume said, 'I'll sing to the lord of this place and we might earn supper and find shelter.' 'The earl himself will decide that,' said Cormac. So soon we stood in front of the Earl of Kildare, Maurice Fitz Thomas Fitzgerald. 'Well,' he said, 'perhaps I could use a good French minstrel. One tires even of Irish songs and the English can't sing anyway.' That night we ate well as honoured guests and Guillaume sang and played. Afterwards, Maurice Fitzgerald said, 'Guillaume, I like what I hear. Will you stay and be my minstrel of honour? Kildare will be a place of music unrivalled in all Ireland.' 'My lord,' said Guillaume, 'before I consent, you must hear our story. When you know it, you may not want us here.' So the earl listened, and when Guillaume finished he laughed and said that a Frenchman and a Welshwoman taking a rise out of the Earl of March's family was the best joke he'd heard that year. So it was agreed. Our home would be the castle. Six months later, Joslin, you were born."

"That means I did live in a castle when I was a baby," he said.

"You did," Rhiannon replied. "Until you were a year and a half."

"I know," said Joslin. "Lately I've had dreams. I saw the castle, I saw you and I heard your voice." He wrinkled his forehead in puzzlement. "But then I had other dreams. I was on a ship. Guillaume was with me. Why? Where were you?"

"Two years," Rhiannon replied. "For two years, Guillaume and I were purely happy. The Earl of Kildare and his household were like nothing I had seen in England or Wales. But those two years were all we had. At the end of them, something terrible happened. Maurice died. His son Gerald became earl. And somehow, James Lamb found us, with a troop of soldiers and a warrant from King Edward of England. They ranged round the castle as if they were starting a siege. Guillaume ran out to James, though I tried to stop him. 'Stay away from us, Lamb,' he shouted. But James laughed. 'I'll wipe that smile off your face,' Guillaume cried. And he took out that dagger of his and slashed James's lips with it."

"Lamb said he was defending an innocent girl when that happened," said Joslin.

"He meant me," said Rhiannon. "Though Guillaume was doing the defending, the king's warrant said my husband took me against my will."

"And Lamb said he was unarmed. My father attacked a defenceless man."

"That man is never unarmed. And he had armed soldiers of the king behind him. He lied to you, as he always does. 'Guillaume, your life is finished now,' he said. Hate dripped out of that voice just as blood dripped from his lips. He demanded three things. He did not want me – I was of no use to him, so he said. He wanted Guillaume as a French spy and you as his own son to bring up as he thought fit. He wanted something else too, he said, of no use to Gerald Fitzgerald, but beyond price to King Edward. The new earl asked what that might be. James only said that Guillaume knew what he meant. Gerald asked for time to consider. 'Till this hour tomorrow,' James answered, and Gerald agreed.

"When he had gone, Gerald said, 'Guillaume, you must fly this place and take the boy with you. There's no time to think, it must be done. Many Irish chieftains owe me favours: Cormac will take you secretly to Cork and there you'll find a ship for France. But you mustn't go without proof from me of who you are.' Gerald called his scribe. An hour later a letter was written and sealed. 'My father's name was well known in France and soon mine will be,' he said. 'This seal will open every door there to you and secure any job as a minstrel. My men are ready and you'll soon be swallowed up in the wilds of

Ireland. Prepare quickly for the journey and say farewell to Rhiannon. One day you'll be back.'

"Those hours were the last time I saw Guillaume. I begged to go with him, but Gerald said, 'It is best if you stay. We will return.' So Guillaume was gone from my life, my only love, except for my child who went with him. As a keepsake, he took the locket as well. Next day, Gerald stood before James Lamb and said, 'I regret to tell the king's warranted representative that the Frenchman escaped in the night. There are reports that he fled north, perhaps to Donegal. You may still catch him.' James Lamb said he would search the castle. 'Please do,' said Gerald. When Lamb found nothing, the last we saw was him going northwards with his soldiers." Rhiannon paused. "Guillaume never came back," she said. "Why not, Joslin?"

"He was Minstrel of Honour in the count's castle in France. Only the count's express permission would let him leave, and he never gave it," Joslin replied. "I can see why. He must have known that Guillaume was a fugitive from the English. He would see it as a duty to protect him and keep his presence there secret. It was cruel luck that the English embassage contained the very two men who were searching for him. Did they know before they came, or was it as big a surprise to them?"

"We'll never know," said Rhiannon. "It doesn't matter now." She looked sad. "All those years I wondered why Guillaume did not come back and take me away. Now I see why. He was protected by a powerful count just as I was protected by a powerful earl. We were both, in a sort of way, prisoners. Some might say for our own good."

"My father never told me about his life," said Joslin. "Never a word. Nothing about Wales or Ireland or James Lamb. I never even knew your name until the anchoress said it. I think he knew that if he did, I'd never have stopped wheedling away at him to take me to you. If we went, I'd be putting us all in new danger. Especially you. I don't think he would have dared take the risk, however much he ached to."

"I wish it hadn't had to be like that," said Rhiannon.

Then a light seemed to glow inside Joslin's mind "It wouldn't always be," he exclaimed. "Now I remember. I know what Guillaume said to me in my dream. I could never hear it before but now I can. 'One day we'll go back,' he said. 'I promise you. One day we'll see your mother, my dearest Rhiannon, again.' But we never did. I know now that if he had lived, one day we would have come to Ireland together. Meanwhile, Guillaume brought me up alone."

Rhiannon looked at him, long and loving. "And very well too," she said. "Very well indeed."

28

"Revenge for the slashed lip. That's why James Lamb killed my father," said Joslin. "He searched for years until he found him." To call Guillaume "my father" without any doubts was like drinking wine. "If I hadn't been hustled off to Cherbourg with my father as he was dying, Lamb would have taken me then and fed me with his lies. No wonder he followed me to Wales."

"I doubt if that was his only reason," said Rhiannon.

"Rhiannon, you said James Lamb wanted a possession beyond price to give to King Edward," said Gyll. "Is it Owain Lawgoch's letter?"

"Yes," Rhiannon replied. "He'd searched the earl's castle so he knew neither Gerald nor I had it. He didn't know if Guillaume had taken it with him. He must have searched Guillaume's room in the castle in France and not found it. He might think Guillaume had given it to you, Joslin. Another reason for following you."

"Now Edmund's dead, will Lamb be out of our lives?" said Joslin.

"He'll never be truly out of our lives," said Rhiannon.

Clouds were rolling in from the west. The sun had gone in and there was a chill in the air. "We must go," said Rhiannon.

It was wonderful to see how Rhiannon, high-born Welsh lady, and Gyll, English jailer's daughter, took to each other so well, though Joslin. He knew why. Their love for him united them and he felt complete, the measure of how far he had come since his grief on *The Merchant of Orwell* as Guillaume's body was committed to the sea.

So he thought as sleep came. He still thought it when pale light woke him. But it was not light from the early sun. A lantern flicked on the floor. A figure, no, two figures, were standing by it. A voice, horribly familiar, spoke. "Awake, are you, Joslin? Well, you've opened your eyes to a worse sight to you than any you might have seen in a nightmare. Even if you're not my son, you'll never be rid of me until I get what I want."

Something flashed in the light. A blade, James Lamb's favourite weapon. A jewel on the handle winked. *It was Guillaume's dagger.*

Who was the second person? Then the terror came. *James held Gyll prisoner and was ready to kill her with Guillaume's dagger.* "Wake your mother," said Lamb. "We have business tonight."

"I was so sure you were dead," Joslin groaned. "Why didn't I kill you?"

"Do you really think that a boy like you could throw me over the edge?" Lamb said. "If you'd looked, you'd have seen me on the ledge below. I dropped down, hid under the overhang and waited. I've got out of worse scrapes than that. Being dead is the best way to hide." His twisted mouth split into that mocking smile. "Wake your mother, Joslin."

But Rhiannon was already awake. She appeared beside Joslin and said, "What do you want with us?"

"You know well," said James Lamb. "There's unfinished business. I need Owain's letter. Guillaume didn't leave it in France. He didn't give it to Joslin – the boy had no idea what I was talking about and I do know innocence when I see it. Olwen didn't have it. That leaves you. Guillaume must have left it with you in Ireland. I know you'd never give it to anyone else. I think you brought it here."

"I can swear to you that I didn't," said Rhiannon.

James Lamb looked round, his eyes glittering. "I feel untruth prickling me," he said.

"I've told no lie," said Rhiannon.

He jerked the blade so it nicked Gyll's neck. She screamed, until he clamped the hand holding the dagger over her mouth. "I'd use this and not blink," he said. "The girl is of no account. Now, the truth."

"I've told you the truth," said Rhiannon.

The noise roused Meic and Mared. They stood, blinking with interrupted sleep. "Don't dare give the alarm," said James. "The girl is a hair's breadth away from death, and I'd go the little extra without a thought."

"I can't tell you any more," cried Rhiannon. "Let Gyll go."

"Not until I have the letter," said James. "I believe what you've told me. Now I want what you haven't told me."

Rhiannon bowed her head for a moment. Then she looked up and said, "Very well. You must follow me."

"Where?" said James cautiously.

"Just follow."

Rhiannon picked up the lantern and led them out of the house. James Lamb, holding Gyll, followed and the others kept up with them, along the path out of the village and past streams flowing loud in the darkness. They were going to the shrine, and Joslin wondered why.

Rhiannon stopped outside the cave. "Guillaume would never take that letter to Ireland or to France. It was for Welshmen and no others, so it stayed in Wales. It is here at the shrine. We entrusted it to Olwen and she promised she would look after it. We'll see if she kept her promise."

"If she didn't, this girl dies," said Lamb.

Rhiannon took the lantern and placed it on the altar. She reached up to the stones shielding the candle, took out the leather bag, which now held the complete relic, and scrabbled with her fingers where it had been. Then, very quietly, she said, "Ah. I see." She took the lantern, stooped and disappeared behind the altar. There was a slight grinding sound, as of stones lifted and replaced. She slowly reappeared holding a letter. They could see the wax seal which closed it.

"Is this what you want?" she said.

James Lamb reached forward. "How should I know?" he said. "I must see for myself. Give it to me."

"Give me Gyll first," said Rhiannon.

"Never," said Lamb. "I won't be tricked again. I do the tricking."

"How if I read it to you?" said Rhiannon. "Can that be a trick?"

"Very well," said Lamb. "Do it."

Rhiannon placed the letter on the altar and broke the seal with a stone. Then she held the letter up and read aloud in Welsh, her voice ringing in the night air. The words were like a magnificent incantation, but all the while, James Lamb was repeating them aloud in English, as if proving to himself that the letter was what she said. His mumbling low voice sounded a second after Rhiannon's – to Joslin it was like a defilement of something perfect.

My people of Wales, whether of Gwynedd, Powys, Ceredigion, Dyfed, Deheubarth, Gwent or Morgannwg, we have lived too long as vassals of the English. I, Owain Lawgoch, last of the Princes of Gwynedd, whose forbears led you in the old time, will lead you again, with a band of true Welshmen and my brothers-in-arms from France, to drive the English away and place on the throne once again a Prince of Wales with native blood running in his veins.

I ask you to join me in this holy and rightful quest. Give me your answer, yea or nay, to the trusted messenger who bears this letter, and on his return I will know whether my countrymen still have strong stomachs and hard sinews for the fight.

Owain Lawgoch
By the grace of God the true Prince of Wales and soon to be Prince of Wales indeed.

She finished and so did James Lamb, still trailing a little behind. "Are you satisfied?" said Rhiannon.

"How do I know that's not a blank sheet?" James Lamb answered. "I've no doubt you can remember every word of it."

"You don't know and you won't see," Rhiannon replied. "You must trust me, take it and give me Gyll. All or nothing."

James Lamb hesitated.

"You have to take the risk, James," Rhiannon said mockingly. "Is it your greatest prize or most painful defeat?"

James Lamb said not a word.

"Come on, James," said Rhiannon. "You live by taking chances. This might prove to be what you've sought for nineteen years. Or it's a trick, I've fooled you and you'll have no great prize to show King Edward."

"Why should I give it to the king?" said James Lamb. "I might take it back to Owain."

Joslin blurted out, "But you spy for King Edward."

245

"Of course I do, Joslin. But Owain thinks I spy for him." That mocking voice again. "And he's right. I'll spy for anybody who pays me. I came to Sycharth because Owain told me to. I don't think he trusted Guillaume after all." Saying this seemed to make his mind up for him. He pushed Gyll into Rhiannon's arms and said, "Give me the letter."

Rhiannon handed it over and said, "Well done, James. You guessed right. Take it and get out of our lives. You've no part in them now."

"Don't worry. I will," he said. But he didn't move. "There's more business yet," he said. He held out the dagger with the jewelled handle. "Your father gave this to you, Joslin," he said. "You should have it back."

Half expecting another trick, Joslin reached for it. Then he stopped. Yes, his father gave him the dagger – but not as he gave the locket and relic. He heard Guillaume's voice: "*Pray God you never need it.*" Well, he'd never used it for killing. But he thought of Ralph Stratford, Roger de Noville's steward, lying dead in a ruined church with that dagger buried in his neck, and Edmund Fitzgrace, murdered with it before his own eyes. It *had* killed. What had James said at the standing stones? "*He was lent that dagger as a sign of the promise he made. But he broke that promise.*" Was it ever Guillaume's to give?

"No," said Joslin. "If Owain Lawgoch lent it, he should have it back."

"Perhaps he will," said James Lamb. "One day." Then he was gone. They heard his voice in the darkness: "*Don't anyone try to follow me.*"

Joslin never saw him again.

They walked slowly back to the town.

"So he's got what he wanted at last," said Joslin.

"Much good will it do him," Rhiannon replied. "Owain Lawgoch had his answer years ago. Wales should look to a better man to be its true prince. I don't regret giving James his letter."

There followed days of peace and happiness in Aberffraw. Joslin could hardly believe that his long travail which had begun that night in the castle in the Cotentin was at last over. At first, he rested. He slept long hours. When awake, he walked, always with Gyll, sometimes with Rhiannon as well, along the shore, through the dunes, across the fields, into the forest. Often he was conscious of Guillaume's spirit walking with them and he knew that this little family would only be split by death.

One day, when they were on their own, sitting where the marram grass shielded them from sharp grains of sand blown in the wind, he said to Gyll, "Shall we marry? I have nothing to offer you except my skill." And Gyll said, "I have no dowry to bring except myself. If you accept that, then of course." When they went back and told Rhiannon she put her arms round them both, cried from joy and gave her blessing.

So the priest married them in his church and joyful were the celebrations in Aberffraw. Then, next day, Rhiannon said, "What shall you do now? Where shall you go?"

Joslin had not thought beyond the moment: his happiness was enough for him. But now he answered. "I don't know." Then: "We'll go where you go. I left France to find you – now I have I shan't leave you."

Rhiannon said, "I shall go back to Ireland. My life, my security, is in Gerald Fitzgerald's castle now."

"Then we'll go with you," said Gyll, before Joslin could.

Rhiannon smiled. "Gerald lost his minstrel of honour when Guillaume left. But with you, he'll have another, just as good. Believe me, he will welcome you both. Life will be good there."

Telling Meic and Mared that they wanted to leave was a heavy thing after all that the people of Aberffraw had done for them. But Meic said, "We'll take you over the sea. Cormac will be waiting and you'll be safe with him." Joslin thought how strangely the flights, escapes, meetings and leavings of his quest echoed his father's years before.

So the crew was brought together and *Newyddion Da* made ready. There was one last night for Joslin to sing. He played every song that had carried him across the land from east to west – *Sir Orfeo, Lai le Freine, Gamelyn, The Carl of Carlisle*. French, English and, haltingly but with growing confidence because his minstrel's memory still worked, Welsh.

Joslin's last act in Wales was to give Herry to Meic. "I'll look after him well," said Meic, patting the piebald horse. "I know you will," said Joslin. "He's served me faithfully and deserves the best." Gyll left Gib also – it was her way of saying thank you. Next morning, at high tide and with a fair wind, they sailed. They watched the shore of Ynis Mon dwindle behind them until they could make it out no more, though Y Wyddfia's great peak stayed visible for longer. Then it was gone, and with it the land through which Joslin had travelled from one sea to another and seen such sights on the way.

They sailed on, beating against a brisk westerly wind over a sparkling sea: a voyage that promised years of gentle happiness ahead. All day, all night they sailed. And as the sun rose next morning, they saw in front of them the great green headland of Howth. Cormac and his men were waiting on the sands, and they knew their voyage was over.

EPILOGUE

Years passed. Owain Lawgoch had still not come back to Wales. But he dreamed on about it. One day, *he thought.* One day . . .

Meanwhile, he was still fighting. And now, in the summer of 1373, he was conducting the long siege of a castle on the banks of the River Gironde, flowing out into the Atlantic. In the castle was an army of Gascons, still loyal to the English. Owain would smoke them all out if it was the last thing he did. But he was in no hurry. Nothing could save them, and out here, in lush fields surrounded by vineyards, the living was easy – even easier now his old friend, after so many, many years, had come back.

"James! James Lamb!" he had cried as that familiar figure, older, disfigured about the face but still unmistakable, had reappeared in his camp one day seven years before.

"Owain, old friend," said James. "It has been so long, but I have never stopped working hard for you. I fear that the French minstrel you sent away on your mission betrayed you. It took me many years to hunt him down. But I did, and now he is dead. I seized from him the letter he was to give to all Welshmen. But he had played you false and unless I had found him he would have given it over to the English. Then I showed it to the foremost Welshmen myself. And Owain, I tell you they ache for the day you will appear off their shores with a mighty army. They ache for the day when they can rally to your flag and send the English packing for ever. It is good tidings that I bring, after all these years."

Owain knelt and gave thanks. to God. Then he embraced James and said, "Welcome, old friend, and with such news too. You were always high in my trust and now, to show you my esteem, I make you my chamberlain and most confidential and wise adviser."

So it was done, and for five years James Lamb lived again as Owain's closest friend. Owain fought many campaigns for the king of France and many more for his own benefit, but the dream of going back to Wales, made more real by James's news, never left him. Little did he know that James still had the letter but kept it close about him

Now, early one morning on a summer's day in 1378, Owain sat on a high hill overlooking the river, waiting for the Gascons to be smoked or starved out of their castle, and watching the wide sea sparkling on the far horizon. He thought of the great days, surely soon to be here, when he would set sail for Wales, with his faithful men and his trusted servant James by his side.

James stood at Owain's shoulder, combing his master's long hair. "Do you see that glorious day ahead, my lord, when you will come into your own at last?" he said.

"I do, James, I do," Owain replied.

"And perhaps it is here already," said James. He hooked his arm round Owain's neck and thrust the dagger with the jewelled and finely wrought handle deep between his ribs. As Owain fell dead, James said, "There. After so very long I have returned your dagger to you as well."

So Owain never led his countrymen in rebellion against the English. That fell later to another Owain, Owain Glyndyr, son of Gruffydd Fychan of Sycharth. And Owain Glyndyr nearly won. But the rebellion failed bravely, as did all rebellions against the English, both before and since.

Meanwhile James Lamb took out the letter again and travelled by secret ways to England where he handed it over to the king and was well paid for all he had done. Afterwards, he lived contentedly for many years, with a wife and children of his own, as if his long pursuit of Joslin de Lay had never happened.

Here ends the sixth and last story concerning Joslin de Lay's journey to Wales and beyond.

AUTHOR'S NOTE

There is a strong historical framework behind this story. Owain Lawgoch, last of the princes of Gwynedd, really existed. He fled to France and the king's court after his family was dispossessed of its lands by the English (and, some say, his father executed), roamed France with his band of renegade Welshmen and fought for the king of France – or anyone else who would pay him well.

Many Welsh people sighed for a new leader and, from about 1350, Owain Lawgoch was the man – a real "king over the water" just as, years later, Bonnie Prince Charlie was for the Scots. He is mentioned in the poem by Y Bergam that Guillaume hears at Sycharth. In 1369 he nearly got an army together to invade (but something stopped it – could it have been an English embassage which called at a castle in the Cotentin?) and in 1378 he met his cruel, underhand death from his supposed best friend.

James (or John) Lamb is mentioned in Froissart's contemporary *Chronicles*, but I first met him in Barbara Tuchman's marvellous book *A Distant Mirror*. I met him again in David Walker's

Medieval Wales and finally in Tony Barr's fascinating *Owen of Wales: the end of the House of Gwynedd.* He appears from nowhere, quickly becomes Owain's most trusted servant and adviser – then stabs him in the back and escapes to England. He may have been a Scotsman and was certainly in the pay of the English. Why, why, *why* should Owain promote this treacherous stranger so quickly? Nobody knows. So I hung the story of the man with the sallow, pockmarked face and twisted lip on this strange, riddling question.

Gruffydd Fychan certainly lived at Sycharth. He was descended from the princes of Powys and was father to Owain Glyndyr, who led the last Welsh rebellion. Sycharth, which the English burned down in the rebellion, exists now only as earthworks – but there is a wonderful, if exaggerated, description of it in Iolo Goch's poem and I've depended a lot on that description for my account of it. If Gruffydd ever had a niece, she was not, to my knowledge, called Rhiannon. The Earls of March ruled the roost in the Welsh Marches, but their kinsman Sir Edmund Fitzgrace, like Rhiannon, exists only in my imagination.

About St Ursula and her companions. It is said she was born in the fourth century AD, daughter of a British king. Not wanting to marry a prince, she was given three years to think about it. With ten women friends, all virgins, she sailed away, ending up on the River Rhine. They reached Cologne in Germany, and here Ursula refused to marry the chief of the Huns, so they were martyred for their Christianity. The ten friends, because of a misreading in a contemporary account, were reputed instead to be a whole thousand. Six hundred years later a tomb was found in Cologne containing a vast number of human bones. At once, everybody assumed they were the bones of Ursula and her thousand companions and they were sent all over Christendom as relics. We now know that assumption was extremely unlikely to be true, but you can't stop people from believing what they want to believe, and certainly many people *wanted* these to be Ursula's bones.

Relics were highly prized. A bone from the body of a saint was said to give its possessor much grace and comfort. This meant that relics became a vast medieval scam. Many were the bits of sheep and cattle which people paid good money for, thinking they were St Peter's big toe or John the Baptist's elbow. Chaucer's Pardoner is the sort of confidence trickster who grew rich on this racket. But some relics were, as far as people in the fourteenth century could tell, genuine, and I certainly intend Guillaume's relic of St Ursula to be, in the eyes of the monks of Shrewsbury Abbey, authentic – even if we would think it certainly wasn't.

Maurice Fitz Thomas Fitzgerald was the fourth Earl of Kildare in Ireland and his son Gerald succeeded him. The Fitzgeralds sound as if they ought to be Norman English barons like the Earls of March (or even of Stovenham). To start with, they were. But three centuries of living in Ireland with a wide sea separating them from kings of England had changed them somewhat. They were becoming more Irish than the Irish – and Fitzgerald is now a common surname in the Republic. Irish people came to look to the earls for leadership against the

English – until the notorious "flight of the earls" centuries later.

The monastery of Strata Marcella was destroyed by Henry VIII's soldiers in the Reformation. Only earthworks are left now. The same fate befell Strata Florida, another great Welsh Cistercian monastery. But one, Valley Crucis, near Llangollen, is left pretty well intact. Aberffraw and Rhosyr in Anglesey were indeed palaces of the ancient princes of Gwynedd: recently there has been much archaeological investigation of Rhosyr and what it was once like is now a lot clearer. I had some of the results of the investigation in mind as I wrote about Edmund's hiding place.

I owe many people thanks for answering my sometimes obscure enquiries so patiently. First, the staffs of several Welsh Tourist and Information Centres, notably Newtown and Holyhead. I have particular reason to thank Andrea Hughes at Holyhead for giving me the name of Meic's ship, *Newyddion Da,* for making me aware of Dwynwen, Anglesey's own saint, and for referring me to Neil Johnstone of the Gwynedd Archaeological and Planning Trust. He in turn gave me magnificent information about excavations of the palaces of Gwynedd, especially Rhosyr.

I also thank an old friend, Peter Hollindale, who put me on to Tony Barr's books, *Medieval Anglesey* and, vital to my own scheme, *Owen of Wales,* mentioned above. These books – and others – led to many hours in the British Library getting a completely unfamiliar background and history as right as I could make it, while still weaving a story round it.

It seems odd to think that when I wrote this book back in 2001 I was not even on the internet. But it almost didn't matter. My son-in-law, Adam Arnell, was superb in getting all sorts of help for me from obscure sites: old maps of Welsh towns, detailed descriptions of the Berwyn Mountains and, most importantly, information about the stone circle of Rhos y Beddau, the existence of which, although it is marked on the Ordnance Survey map, I was beginning to doubt. A last-minute piece of news from the internet about when Maurice Fitzgerald, Earl of Kildare, died and his son Gerald succeeded him prevented me from making something of a howler at the very end. Thank you so much, Adam.

However, I have no doubt that, in spite of the help I've been given by all these willing people, there are plenty of howlers left in this story – and the others in this series. If there are, they are all down to me.

DENNIS HAMLEY

About the Author

Dennis Hamley's first novel, *Pageants of Despair*, was first published by Andre Deutsch in 1974. Since then he has written over eighty books, mainly for children and young adults. These include *The War and Freddy* (shortlisted for the Smarties Prize), *Hare's Choice, Spirit of the Place, Out of the Mouths of Babes, Ellen's People* (published in the USA as *Without Warning*), which is set in World War 1, and *Divided Loyalties*, set in World War 2. He has published with Scholastic, OUP, Franklin Watts, Walker Books and several others. He has been published in the USA by Delacorte, SG Philips, Candlewick Press and Paul Dry Books. Many of his books have been translated into other languages.

The six books in *The Long Journey of Joslin de Lay* sequence were first published by Scholastic between 1998 and 2001, in the Point Crime series. They have been translated into German, published by Arena Verlag, and Italian, published by Mondadori. Dennis has always been interested in the Middle Ages. His very first book, published in 1962, consisted of modern adaptations of medieval Miracle Plays, *Three Towneley Plays,* (Heinemann) and his very first novel, *Pageants of Despair*, was about the Wakefield Mystery Cycle.

He now writes mainly as an independent author. His website is dennishamley.co.uk

Also in Joslin Books

Colonel Mustard in the Library with the Candlestick
Out of the Deep: stories of the supernatural
Yan Tan Tethera: six stories and a very tiny novel

Bright Sea, Dark Graves
1. *The Guns of St Thérèse*
2. *Nightmares of Invasion*

Also in *The Long Journey of Joslin de Lay*
1. *Of Dooms and Death*
2. *A Pact with Death*
3. *Hell's Kitchen*
4. *A Devil's Judgement*
5. *An Angel's Curse*

26228742R00162

Made in the USA
Columbia, SC
07 September 2018